The Healer
Jean Brashear

D1305094

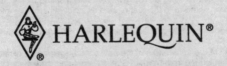

HARLEQUIN®

TORONTO • NEW YORK • LONDON
AMSTERDAM • PARIS • SYDNEY • HAMBURG
STOCKHOLM • ATHENS • TOKYO • MILAN • MADRID
PRAGUE • WARSAW • BUDAPEST • AUCKLAND

ISBN 0-373-71105-0

THE HEALER

Copyright © 2003 by Jean Brashear.

Printed in U.S.A.

Enduring friendship is one of life's true treasures.

To Pam Winget Parker, friend since we were toddlers,
for memories spanning a lifetime…with heartfelt thanks
for encouraging my writing ventures.

To Charlotte Hill Greene, who shared mothers and sisters,
Camp Fire and convertibles and crazy impulses.

To Nancy Smith Munger, with whom I stood in the back row
with the boys and without whom I would never have
survived junior high.

And to my long-lost friend Dee Parkins, with deep gratitude
for having the courage to find me again.

All of you make my life richer because you're in it.

ACKNOWLEDGMENTS

I owe thanks to many for help with research for this book. Occupational therapist Kristen Kitchen generously spent hours explaining radial nerve damage and rehabilitation; O.T. Joanna Van Hoove first grabbed my storyteller's attention when speaking of what makes a good (or difficult) rehab patient. My brother-in-law Steve Brashear gave me insights into life in the Special Forces and the unique members who are their medics; Rachel Harris and Janie Aguillera guided me on colloquial Spanish phrases, and Rachel graciously shared her memories of Mexican-American traditions.

To Lupita Barrera, thanks for introducing me to *curanderismo* and sharing your Mama Lalita with me. I'm grateful, also, to three wonderful resources on the tradition: Eliseo Torres's works, *The Folk Healer* and *Green Medicine*, and Elena Avila's excellent and insightful book, *Woman Who Glows in the Dark*.

All errors made or liberties taken are my own.

PROLOGUE

Dallas

"DR. MALONE, that was amazing." The intern's eyes shone. "It's true what they say—you're the best."

"Thanks." Caroline Malone stripped off her mask and cap, casting the eager young man a faint, tired smile. The adrenaline that had kept her going for too much of the fourteen-hour surgery had vanished, leaving her legs rubbery in its wake. She still had to talk to the family, and right now all she wanted to do was slide to the floor and sleep around the clock.

"If people could see what we see, they'd take better care of themselves," the intern muttered. Then he beamed again. "I've decided. I'm going into cardio for sure. I want to be like you and save lives."

Feeling less like a hero than ten miles of bad road at the moment, still she hesitated to dampen his enthusiasm by saying so.

Before she could answer, the door swung wide, and Judd Carter stood in the opening. "Miracle Malone strikes again, I hear." He shot a look at the intern and leaned closer to Caroline, speaking low. "It must get crowded in the surgical suite, making room for you and that halo."

Caroline had learned not to expect any better from the man who'd come to Mercy Hospital anticipating that they'd all fall down on their knees and worship his greatness. She'd worked hard to become the best, and she refused to concede her position to him and his Harvard degree.

His response had been to try seduction. His blond hair and blue eyes had had the nursing staff panting, but Caroline hadn't been interested. Still wasn't. No man would turn her into the clinging creature her mother had been. No wonder Caroline's father had left.

Of course, he'd left her, too.

"It was a team effort. Excuse me, Judd." She pushed her way past where he blocked the door. "I have to speak with the family."

"Ah, yes—to take your bow. By all means, Queen Caroline."

She knew what the staff called her, but only he did it to her face. What name they gave her didn't matter as long as they did the work. She didn't demand any more of others than she did of herself.

You didn't become the best by doing things halfway.

Refusing to rise to the bait, she gave him her back, focusing, instead, on what she'd say to the loved ones of a man who'd died twice on the table.

EIGHTEEN HOURS LATER, the rest of the weekend was all hers. She turned off the two-lane blacktop road ten miles south of Dallas and drove between the thick cedar posts that signaled the boundaries of the farm where she boarded her horse. Winter still clasped the dry, pale beige grass to its bosom, but the air was crisp, the sky an endless baby blue dotted with cotton-puff clouds.

Nothing beat a good long ride to work out the tension of a week like this one. Yesterday's procedure had had enough drama, even for her.

But she was much in demand and loved her work. She just needed some exercise—she'd had to miss her run yesterday and overslept this morning.

Rolling her neck, she winced. A massage wouldn't hurt, either.

She finished saddling Star King and vaulted onto his back, needing the release of the wind through her hair, the tang of cedar spicing the earthy richness of country air. "Okay, big boy—you're ready to run and so am I."

Caroline smiled as his powerful muscles burst into action. They rode in tune like lovers. The week slipped away, her energy rebounding. Laughing out loud for the joy of the freedom this magnificent horse gave her, she closed her eyes for a split second to savor it.

A jackrabbit darted.

Star King shied.

Caroline shifted her weight to counteract his momentum—

Too little, too late. She lost her grip on the reins, sailed through the air. Slammed to the ground on her right side.

Pain exploded in her arm.

Then…only darkness.

CHAPTER ONE

Davis Mountains, West Texas

IN THE ROOM WARM with candlelight, fragrant with soothing lavender and pungent rosemary, the child slid into Diego Montalvo's waiting hands. *"Milagro,"* he murmured in Spanish. That hands once honed to kill should now bring forth life still humbled him.

His grandmother's hand settled on his shoulder. Always, her touch brought warmth and comfort. "Each child a miracle," she agreed. "Every time."

There had been many of them for her, Diego knew. She had delivered every child born in this valley for over sixty years now. He rose to his feet. "A little girl," he said to the exhausted mother and the father, whose face outshone the sun. *"Un tesoro."* A treasure. A lucky child to be so wanted.

Supported by the husband seated behind her, the mother reached for her baby, tears rolling down her cheeks. She touched every finger, every toe.

"They're all there," Diego teased. "I counted."

The father looked up from his new family. "Diego...*la señora*..." He shook his head. "It is not possible to tell you—"

Diego clapped one hand on the man's shoulder, clearing his throat. "Care for them well. That's thanks enough."

His grandmother stepped forward. "Drink this," she urged the new mother. "A decoction of basil, honey and nutmeg. It will help expel the placenta."

Diego moved past her to examine the baby girl. Strong responses, breathing clear, everything normal. "She looks good, little mother." He smiled. "You've done well."

The next few minutes were busy ones as they waited for the umbilical cord to cease pulsing so it could be cut, cleansed the child and returned her safe to the arms of her mother. His grandmother hung back, letting him do most of it, though he would have to deliver many, many more children before his was the smooth ballet of her movements. *Curandera* for the entire valley, she was the only health care for many miles around. She healed the sick, brought forth life and comforted the dying, but her strength was waning in her eighty-third year.

At last they were done. "Mama Lalita," he said to his grandmother. "Let's sit down." He knew better than to suggest that only she take a rest, though energy rolled through him in waves.

The grateful father brought them iced tea and conversed with them under the lone tree in his front yard. He kept glancing back toward the house, and finally Diego laughed. "Go on," he urged. "Be with them. We'll leave in a few minutes. I'll come by to check on them tomorrow unless you need me earlier."

Diego's gaze lingered as the young man left. Had he ever thought he'd reach almost forty without holding his own child in his arms? Too many years spent living on the edge, too busy reveling in danger and adrenaline to even consider settling down. Then, with stunning swiftness, he'd been fighting to live. To walk again.

"Is your hip hurting you, *m'ijo?*" his grandmother asked. "Kneeling is hard."

He shrugged. "The payoff is worth it."

"You bring them hope. They know they will be cared for when I am gone."

Dread sliced deep. "I'm not you, *Abuela*. I don't have your gift."

"Look at me," she ordered, dark eyes flashing. "You are wrong. It is your destiny. These are your people. You are a *curandero,* whether you believe it or not. Our way came down from the Aztecs. It has been in your blood for centuries. We are healers, made so to help others learn to live in harmony with self and nature. A wounded soul is as deadly as torn flesh. You know this—" She touched a finger to his heart. "In here, you feel the truth."

"I've been gone a long time. I'm a medic, nothing more."

She sank against her chair, her eyes filled with sorrow. "You give yourself too little credit. Your powers will outstrip mine." She sighed. "I understand that it is hard. You fight the battle of those born into two worlds."

"Belonging in neither," he added.

"Diego Cameron Montalvo, your mother does not deserve that. She made certain you never had to choose. She opposed her own family after my son's death, refusing to make you or your brother turn your back on your father's people."

Diego thought of his slender, blond, blue-eyed mother and smiled. She and this tiny woman beside him looked nothing alike but shared a ferocity far beyond the size of either.

"You're right. Jesse and I did that all by ourselves." The knowledge still shamed him.

"Ah, *m'ijo*," she sighed. "You have fought too many battles. Let go. Your path is no longer war. Be at peace. Know that within you is all you need, all these people need."

He loved this woman more than his life. Always, always she had been there. Always she brought comfort and calm. "I watch. I listen and try to learn. As to the rest—" He spread his fingers, shrugging. "Let's hope your faith remains stronger than my doubts. Now—" He shot her a smile and rose. "Let me escort you home before I do one last check on the cabin of our new guest.''

She clasped his face between the bony hands that had helped so many. ''You will not disappoint these people who need you, Diego. Of this I am sure. It is why you came here to finish healing. You were called. This is where you belong.''

Diego helped her rise, knowing only that what he could bring to the people of this valley he had once been so eager to leave, he would gladly give.

But far from sure it would be enough.

YOUR PROGRESS HAS STALLED OUT, Caroline. You refuse to see it, but you're risking everything. I'm going to insist that you take a month off from therapy. Her occupational therapist's voice reverberated inside her head as the miles rolled past the car window.

She didn't have time to take a month off. She had patients who needed her. Her partners couldn't handle the increased workload. She should be back in the surgical suite, back where she knew who she was. She was the best. She'd worked hard for it, she couldn't be a—

Cripple.

Will I ever do surgery again? she'd asked Don Henderson.

No soft-soaping, right? Don had stared at her for a long time. *I can't tell you yet. You can definitely regain the use of the hand, but the kind of fine motor skills needed for cardiac surgery? It could go either way.*

No. Unacceptable. For a surgeon who operated on hearts, nothing less than total restoration of her dexterity would do. Already, four months had gone by. Don said it could take months longer.

Her patients didn't have months. Colin Langdon had a new child, a life to live. Martha Powers wanted to see her youngest grandchild graduate. The children Caroline treated pro bono needed her talents.

Judd Carter wouldn't care enough. He wouldn't take on the cases that didn't serve his ambition. Her patients would be so worried, and she was—

Helpless. Damn it. Only barely did she check the urge to bang on the car window as she looked out at the mountains that had emerged after endless miles of nothing but cactus and dirt.

Once she'd have marveled, filled with energy for exploring. Right now she only wanted to be someone else. Somewhere else than some godforsaken rustic cabin that hospital administrator Sam Calvert had leased, hoping to buy his rainmaker some peace.

His rainmaker didn't want to be here. She wanted escape. Wanted to hit the road and jam down on the accelerator, to drive far and fast and outrun the wreckage her life had become in the wake of her accident.

"Ma'am, are you all right back there?" The driver looked concerned.

Caroline glanced down at the hand lying in her lap, the brace on her wrist. *Work, damn you. Get well. Please.*

But aloud she only said, "Yes. I'm fine."

And returned to staring at the landscape to which she'd been exiled. She'd traveled the corridors from Dallas to Houston to Austin a lot, had been to San Antonio many times. Far West Texas had never been a part of the state she'd cared to visit, assuming it to be barren and arid.

Much of it was exactly that—a monochromatic vista, endless acres of dirt dotted by plants as much gray as green.

But the sky felt...enormous. As though she could breathe fresh air deep into her lungs. It was almost overpowering, this huge blue bowl of sky, punctuated here and there by pale traces of cloud.

Now they were winding into mountains unlike any she'd seen. Not grand like the Rockies, not blanketed with thick forest. These trees were scattered, casting fine, lacy shadows on the ground. The greens grew more vivid, but still there was so much...sky.

Caroline recalled that the MacDonald Observatory was located here because the skies were clear of the artificial blaze by which man ignored circadian rhythms and led a dual existence.

She saw few signs that man existed at all. For a

moment she let herself imagine racing Star King over the flat ground they'd covered. Climbing these slopes, discovering what was around the next bend.

This was an odd, ancient place. The past still lived here, she thought.

But she was a city girl, accustomed to the rich, endlessly fascinating world of man's innovations. She loved art galleries and experimental theater and fine dining.

Somehow, though, she had to survive a month in this place. Had to prove to Sam Calvert and Don Henderson that she'd rested enough so that they'd let her get back to work.

While the parade of patients in need of her care marched through her heart in jackboots, Caroline leaned her head back against the seat and wondered how she'd ever survive exile in this harsh and foreign land.

DIEGO HEARD the car tires as he tightened the pipes under the sink one last time. He heard a woman's voice speaking in quick, authoritative tones. A man answered, then steps sounded on the porch.

Rising to his feet, Diego wiped his hands on a rag from his tool chest, walked to the door and opened it just as a slender blonde reached for the knob.

Annoyance flitted across her forehead. "I was told this was my cabin."

She was one of those too-thin, driven women, he

thought. Shaggy cap of hair, no makeup. Always in a hurry to get there, unable to enjoy the journey. "If you're Caroline Malone, you're right."

Green eyes sharpened. "And who might you be?"

Diego grinned. "I might be anyone."

She cast a glance at the grease on his hands, then her brow cleared. "Ah. They said there was a caretaker. That must be you." She turned to the driver. "Just leave my bags there. Mr.—?" She glanced back.

"Montalvo. Diego Montalvo."

One quick nod. "Mr. Montalvo can take them inside for me. Here—" She handed several bills to the driver.

A decent tipper, it seemed. Even if she no doubt considered the driver invisible.

Without further goodbye, she peered past Diego. "Is there a problem?"

Only that you're wound tight as a spring ready to pop. "No, no problem. The cabin hasn't been used in a couple of months, and the pipes have a lot of years on them. Just making sure everything is ready."

A brisk nod and she brushed past him. Inside the cabin, she glanced around the single room that was living room-dining room-kitchen.

"Bedroom and bath are through there," he said, trying to see the cabin through her eyes. *Rustic* might be the kindest word she'd use, but the place was clean and sound. People didn't come out here for the Ritz.

Although, he amended, maybe this one would wish for it.

She raked the fingers of her left hand through her hair, but her right hand was wrapped in a brace, held close to her body.

"You want some help with your luggage?" he asked.

Absently, she nodded, then walked through the bedroom door.

You're welcome. He tossed the rag onto his toolbox. When he picked up her bags, one weighed a ton. Carrying them inside, he asked, "Where do you want them?"

She emerged through the doorway. "That one—" she pointed to the heavy one "—stays in here. The other one in the bedroom."

He shrugged. "The weather's not very cold yet, except at night. You got a whole winter wardrobe in here?"

Her nostrils pinched. "Not that it's any of your business, but those are books and magazines."

He glanced at the much lighter, smaller case. What kind of woman brought so few clothes and so much to read?

"Professional reading," she said. "I have to keep up." For a moment, something clouded her gaze.

"What kind of profession?" he asked.

Lost in thought, she took a moment to answer. "What? Oh—I'm a surgeon. Cardiac. That's the heart."

"Yeah," he answered. "I do speak English. They thought it was important at my college."

She didn't smile. "Then why are you— Never mind."

"Why am I taking care of a mountain cabin?" He shrugged. "Getting by. What are you doing here? Don't cardiac surgeons prefer vacationing in places like Cozumel or Aspen?"

Instead of the retort he expected, he saw her shoulders hunch slightly. Something broken darkened those remarkable eyes just for a moment, then her back went ramrod stiff. "I was in a riding accident and suffered nerve damage to my hand. I've been undergoing occupational therapy, but—" She looked away. "My therapist felt a break was necessary, someplace quiet."

But she didn't think so; that much was obvious. Her look was a mixture of resignation and anger and—

Fear. That was what he saw. She was afraid; that was why she was so brittle. This was a woman running scared.

Compassion stirred. "Well, you've come to the right place for that. These mountains are easy on the mind."

"My mind is fine," she snapped. Then she glanced at him. "I'm sorry. It's not your fault. I'm being rude." Her voice wavered. "It wasn't my choice. I'm needed there. I have patients who will die if I don't—" She whirled away, waving behind her. "Just leave the bags where they are. I'll get them later." She fumbled through her purse, the movements of her left hand awkward.

Susto, Mama Lalita would diagnose. A wounding of the spirit far greater than whatever had happened to her hand. This woman needed more than physical care, but someone like her would be the last one to accept it.

Diego had her mark. She, as he had three years earlier, faced losing the life she'd made for herself. Cardiac surgeons were jet jockeys, arrogant enough to take the organ that ruled life or death into their hands. A woman in their ranks would have to be driven. Getting there meant years of intense work and competition. If she was any good, she would have had to surmount many obstacles on her way.

And for her, like him, in the space of a breath, all had changed.

His medical knowledge told him that her odds weren't good. The fine motor skills required for any surgery, much less heart surgery, had to be the best. His own months in physical therapy had shown him just how seldom people returned exactly to their original state.

The healer in him sized up her battle and wanted to help.

The hardened soldier knew that she would refuse it.

So the owner of the cabin decided to let things go for now and simply keep an eye on her. He picked up her bags. "I've got a few minutes."

When she pulled bills from her purse, though, and held them out, all of those men growled as one, "Forget it."

THAT NIGHT, after the fourth reading of the same sentence, Caroline threw the magazine aside and leaped to her feet. Pacing from sofa to front door and back again, she scanned the bookshelves on which she'd arranged her reading list, but nothing beckoned.

She turned in a circle, surveying the room, wanting to block out how foreign it all was, wishing she'd brought something, anything, of hers to make this place feel familiar.

An impersonal hotel room might have been easier. This cabin was too homey, furnished with care if not a lot of money. The arms of the avocado plaid sofa were a little threadbare, the green-and-blue woven rugs on the floor faded with time. The small round maple kitchen table, with its four chairs, sported nicks and scratches. In the center of it sat a stunning clay pot fired in dramatic glazes of deep green and cobalt. She traced the curves at its base. Whoever had made this was an artisan of rare skill. It was both earthy and ethereal, sensual and grounded.

In it someone had placed flowers and some kind of pungent greenery. The caretaker? He didn't seem the type for flowers. Too big, too rugged. These weren't from any florist, though—they'd been picked from someone's garden, a garden perhaps like one she'd almost forgotten her mother having, back before her father left and cast their lives into chaos.

Zinnias, that was what the flowers were. Bright round faces in reds and oranges. She had a quick memory of them, sprouting from her mother's compost pile one year. *You can't kill these things, honey.*

If only her mother had been as hardy as a zinnia, instead of so damn weak she'd leave her three daughters at the mercy of fate and a system that could crush them.

She spied the ancient radio with relief. Desperate for respite from her thoughts and the endless silence, she switched it on. Guitars and a rich baritone sang a song of heartache, of love gone wrong.

Country music. Caroline snorted at the caretaker's taste. Definitely not her cup of tea, especially not tonight. Jazz was her game, that and Broadway show tunes. She extended one hand to the dial, but before she could change it, something slow and sweet and sad reached down inside and grabbed her, crowding her throat.

A man so in love with a woman he'd weather any storm, never leave her side. Were there really men like that? Did such love exist?

Maybe for others, or maybe not at all. Certainly not for her, not that she'd seen. She'd loved her father with everything in her, had done her best to make him as proud as if she'd been that son he'd so wanted. When he'd walked away without a word, he'd broken the part of her that knew how to trust.

But she'd survived. She'd thrived. Look how far she'd come; look who she'd been—

Dread's cold fist crushed her heart. It couldn't be over. She had too much to do yet. If she couldn't, if the worst happened—

No. The worst wouldn't happen. She wouldn't let it. She was strong, not weak like her mother. Ivy had once said nothing would ever defeat Caroline—

Ivy. Caroline sank to the sofa, thinking of her sister. Missing her. Four years younger, Ivy had taken it hard when their mother had died and they'd been split up. She'd fought for them to stay together, swearing she'd take care of both Caroline and little Chloe, barely four at the time. She'd pleaded with Caroline to help her make their case, but Caroline had known they were defeated from the start. No judge would let a thirteen-year-old and a seventeen-year-old raise a small child.

Then, vivid as the day it had happened, Caroline saw again Ivy's blue eyes bright with barely stemmed tears as she tried to convince Chloe to go with the nice lady. The social worker had been frank that Chloe stood a good chance of being adopted but that few families wanted to take on teenagers.

Caroline had wanted to cry, sure, but she was the strong one, the one who coped. She'd held Ivy as Ivy sobbed after Chloe was gone; her own eyes had burned as, in turn, she'd watched Ivy leave. She'd marched to her own foster home without emotion, already knowing that at the first opportunity, she'd be gone.

And she had. Four months and two homes later, Caroline was on her own. She'd been smart and careful and avoided the streets. Worked lousy jobs, gone from community college to a full-fledged university, where she'd found her path. Studied hard and hocked herself up to her eyeballs all the way through medical school, to graduate first in her class.

But accomplishing so much had meant no time to dwell on the past. After one failed attempt to find her sisters, she'd grown accustomed to being solitary, and seldom allowed herself a thought of her only kin left.

If, on graduation day, she'd longed to have someone there, she hadn't dwelled on it. One day, perhaps, she'd look again for her sisters—one day, when her life was back on track.

And if, on this lonely dark night, Caroline wished a little for the comfort of family, for the coddling at which Ivy had excelled, even so young, well...she had survived a lot of lonely nights.

She would make it through this night. And the next.

Until she had her life in order again.

CHAPTER TWO

IN THE MORNING, hope grabbed a foothold again. She would beat this setback, just as she'd beaten all the others in her life. She'd be back in the surgical suite in no time.

That settled, Caroline walked out on the porch and began her prerun stretches. She'd finished Don's routine—exercises with the therapeutic putty, such as squeezing the tacky clay with her hand; making it into a tight doughnut shape around her fingers, then spreading them wide. She'd fastened the wide yellow plastic Therabands to the doorknob and rowed to strengthen her shoulders. But she couldn't let everything else get out of shape. She'd need her stamina more than ever after this extended layoff. Daylong surgical procedures were not for sissies.

Motion across the pasture caught her eye—a beautiful bay mare and her foal. The baby danced around his mother, little kicks with his hind legs, butts against her side. Finally the mare relented, and the baby began to nurse.

Within Caroline, faint longing flickered. She'd

never built her life around fantasies of family as Ivy had almost from birth, but she guessed she'd always assumed she'd get to that somewhere along the way. She was thirty-six and certainly not out of the game, but she had to admit that motherhood didn't look likely. The last semiserious relationship she'd had was two years ago. Many men were intimidated by her success or couldn't tolerate the demands of her career; so be it. She had what she wanted most: her work and her independence. If the rest of it came, fine. If not...

Her only focus had to be resuming her practice. Not once in her life had she failed to achieve any goal she set; she would not start now.

Shoving away maudlin thoughts, Caroline finished her stretches and headed out for her run. Crisp, cool air stung her skin, a welcome change from the dense, suffocating heat she'd left behind her. Confidence gained new ground as waking muscles burned. For too long she hadn't been allowed to run for fear of jarring her arm, of disturbing the outrigger splint keeping her fingers from curling into a claw. It had been one more loss to grieve, one more piece of her ordered life ripped out.

Grief slid away on this bright morning, and in its place, optimism expanded a chest too long weighted with despair. Caroline picked up her pace.

Her head felt a little light, but she pushed herself, giddy and young once more, full of life and vigor.

She calculated that she could reach the little house she saw up ahead in less than a minute, and she closed off all other thoughts to concentrate on meeting her goal, proud to be able to rely on her body again.

The seconds counted down in her head, and she kicked up one more notch when she sensed she wouldn't make it. A dark arrow speared through her vision, but she ignored it. Ten more yards to the gate—

Her legs buckled without warning. Caroline fell to her knees, throwing her left arm out and tucking in her vulnerable right hand, fighting to keep from toppling.

Adrenaline shot through her system. Heart pounding, she closed her eyes, trying to steady her breathing.

"Are you hurt, child?"

Caroline jolted.

"Sh-h…let me look at you." The old woman's voice eased something inside her. Serenity was there, deep and sure. And compassion.

"My…hand," she managed, still bent over, shaking. "If I hurt it—" Terror rolled over her in waves.

Warm fingers stroked her forehead. "One deep breath, slow and steady," the voice urged. "Let go of your fear. It has no place here."

For the life of her, Caroline couldn't explain why she believed the woman, but she did. She was the expert, the medical professional, but at this moment, the quaking child inside her heard certainty in this old woman's voice. Terror released its stranglehold.

"That's right," the woman soothed. "Will you let me touch your hand?"

Caroline opened her eyes and looked into a lined brown face that spoke of pain and deep knowing, of calm strength and peace. Sharp eyes that would never be fooled but did not lie, either, she thought. All the same, she kept her hand tucked close. "There's no need. I'm fine," she said, voice still shaky.

"If you wish," the old woman said, the soul of patience. She placed one hand on top of Caroline's head.

Extraordinary warmth flowed over Caroline. Without thinking, she allowed the breath she'd been holding to escape, and the sensation slid farther into her body.

For a few seconds, nothing mattered but this stillness that suffused her. She wanted to draw it into her lungs, to fill her belly with it, to curl up in its shelter and hide away until—

A dog barked, and Caroline's eyes snapped open. "Who are you?"

The old woman frowned in concentration and shook her head once. She passed her hand over Caroline's face, hovering a bare inch from her skin, then moved down to scan her torso. Over the center of

Caroline's chest, she paused, her frown deepening. *"Susto,"* Caroline thought was the word she muttered.

What the—

Caroline's muscles bunched, readying to sit up, to move away from this odd woman.

The old woman's eyes popped open. Within their depths, something ancient peered back at Caroline, and she shivered.

The woman sat back on her heels. "You protect your hand as fiercely as you protect your heart." She laid her hand on Caroline's shoulder. "But there are deep wounds that need healing or you will never reclaim your life."

"Who are you?" Caroline persisted.

"Only an old woman who has seen much in her years." She smiled. "Would you care for a cup of tea on this bright morning?" She struggled to rise.

Caroline stood and extended her good hand to assist. As quickly as possible, she pulled away. "I don't—thank you, but I should be going. I must—"

"What is your hurry? Will the day not be long enough for many things?" In the dark eyes, Caroline saw a twinkle.

She stopped in her tracks. Exhaled. "Sorry. Force of habit, always racing to fight the next fire. If it's not too much trouble, a cup of tea would be nice."

The tiny, ancient woman's smile widened.

"Good. We shall enjoy this lovely new morning and all its blessings."

Caroline was not religious. Having given up on God long ago, she found that talk of spiritual matters made her uncomfortable; yet somehow, coming from this woman, the word *blessings* didn't seem dogma but instead a simple acknowledgment that life could bring small joys.

When was the last time she stopped to notice such joys? As she followed the woman through her gate, a tiny flare of gladness rose, a spark of well-being. She cradled it to her chest the way she protected her vulnerable hand.

An ancient dog, fat and brown, gray at the muzzle, rose on unsteady legs to greet the woman, then peered past her to Caroline.

"A new friend, Dulcita." The old woman looked at Caroline. "Her name means a small sweet, a name my husband gave her when she was tiny enough to fit in his palm. As you can see from her figure, she is indulged perhaps a little more than is strictly necessary. My Diego taught her to love treats early in her life, and she adores them still."

"Diego?" Caroline asked. "The caretaker?"

"Is that what he told you?" The old woman smiled, shaking her head. "No, not the same Diego. That one is my grandson, named after my late husband."

What did the smile mean? But Caroline clung to

her manners even as she mused. "I'm sorry for your loss."

"As am I," the woman said. "But he is still alive in me. He has been gone for fourteen years, but he comes to me in my dreams each night."

Her voice was soft and tender when she spoke of him, but Caroline heard no defeat. She glanced around at the neat, small gray stucco house, with its bright turquoise door and coral shutters. The vegetable garden brimmed with shiny red tomatoes and deep green peppers. Tall lavender hollyhocks and yellow climbing roses lined the fence. This woman obviously missed her husband but wasn't lost without him as her mother had been when her father left. Everywhere Caroline looked, she saw life and abundance, hope and care.

"You haven't let his loss break you," she said.

The old woman's eyes widened. "It will be a glorious moment when I can go to him, but I cannot leave yet. There is still one thing left for me to do."

Silence fell. The old woman did not explain herself, and Caroline felt it wrong to pry. She glanced around for a change in topic. "You have so many plants. I don't recognize most of them. I'm not much of a gardener," she said. "I'm Caroline Malone, by the way." She held out her left hand. Self-conscious, she started to withdraw it.

The old woman clasped her hand and smiled. Again, Caroline felt that odd warmth.

"And I am Adelaida Montalvo. You are a doctor, are you not?"

Caroline nodded. "How did you know?"

A small shrug. "Diego mentioned it. I thought perhaps you might enjoy seeing my medicinal plantings."

"You're into herbal medicine?" She stifled a frown. She didn't want to offend Mrs. Montalvo, but she'd had her share of patients who'd compromised their health by self-diagnosing with herbal supplements for serious medical conditions.

Adelaida continued. "It is a tradition of my people going back to the Aztecs. At a time when European medicine was little more than butchery, the Aztec culture had a sophisticated understanding of the weaving of body, soul, spirit and emotions necessary to maintain and heal the body. This medicine is called *curanderismo*. When the Spaniards came, influenced by the Moors, their traditions were incorporated, as were the healing practices of the Africans brought over as slaves. Over time, the Catholic faith, too, made its mark. *Curanderismo* is the medicine of the people, and it is still practiced today."

"I've never heard of it."

"Not surprising." The old woman smiled. "Western medical schools have only recently begun to explore alternative methods of healing. My grandson was skeptical until he began to study with me.

He'd seen me work before, of course, but a child takes little note of such things. The roots of modern medicine lie in these plants.'' She gestured. ''That one there, with the spire of bell-shaped flowers? That is foxglove, the source of digitalis. This one—'' she pointed to a tall green plant with oval leaves ''—I'm sure you recognize as basil.'' She plucked a leaf and brought it to Caroline's nose.

''I've cooked with it—not that I cook much,'' Caroline admitted. ''But I've never seen it growing. It's pretty.''

''Yes, it is. One of my most useful plants. It can be used to stop cramping and it works as a sedative. In a concentrated tea, it is a gargle for sore throats or for sores inside the mouth.'' She stopped by another plant. ''This is *manzanilla,* though you may have heard it by the name chamomile.''

Chamomile reminded Caroline of genteel Victorian ladies in old English novels. ''What is its purpose?''

Mrs. Montalvo studied her. ''I will make you a tea. It will help you sleep. By itself, it is too bitter, but I combine others with it.'' She frowned. ''You have not rested well in a very long time, have you?''

Caroline turned away, uncomfortable under the gaze of those too-knowing eyes. ''I guess I'll get plenty of that now,'' she muttered.

The old woman didn't respond but continued her tour, stopping here and there to pull weeds as she explained the names and uses of various plants. Though Caroline doubted the effectiveness of any of them compared with modern pharmaceuticals, she didn't want to argue the merits of medical protocols with someone so kind and well-meaning.

Their slow progress soothed her. Mrs. Montalvo didn't speak simply to chatter; long silences passed in which the only sound was that of a mockingbird's song, the soft nicker of a horse, the constant brush of the wind. She saw zinnias again, learned that the greenery with them on her table was rosemary.

Caroline began to help, finding the loamy scent of earth agreeable, the feel of the soil more enjoyable than she would have ever imagined. As they touched sage and lavender and rosemary, a lavish, constantly changing bouquet perfumed the air, sometimes sweet, sometimes sharp, always pungent.

She made tentative efforts to use her right hand. She could grip now, to some extent, but the radial nerve injury meant that she couldn't extend her fingers, so she released things only by using her left hand to remove items from the clasp of her right. Not expecting to need it, she'd left her brace off this morning, making progress slow and awkward.

Nonetheless, she found herself relaxing by inches, working side by side in the sunshine with this remarkable woman. If her colleagues could see her now, dirt under her fingernails and caking her knees, they wouldn't believe it was Queen Caroline.

Nor could she herself believe it. This was a way of life completely outside her experience. She exhaled, the tightness in her shoulders dissolving beneath the rays of the sun, the richly scented air, the deep and lasting peace this woman exuded.

Into this buzzing, drifting quiet came the sound of hoofbeats. Like a landlocked sailor at the first sound of waves, Caroline stirred to sudden attention. The harrowing results of her accident had not made her fear horses; she knew the fault had been her inattention, not Star King's blunder. The biggest loss after her career was having to stop riding. She missed it every day.

In the distance, she saw a big man on an Appaloosa stallion, the two strong and sure and beautiful in the crisp morning light. Mesmerized, she hadn't realized how still she'd become until she jolted when the old woman spoke.

"On horseback, Diego forgets the ghosts that haunt him. When he rides is the only time he is whole and young again."

Diego? The caretaker? *Is that what he told you?* she remembered the old woman asking. Who was this man who fixed pipes, who studied herbal medicine, who rode as though born to it?

"Mrs. Montalvo," she began.

"Adelaida, please."

Caroline nodded. "Adelaida, what did you mean?

He said he was the caretaker. They told me there would be—''

Adelaida smiled. ''Did he say those words or did he simply let you believe them?''

She'd been made a fool. ''What do you mean?''

The small brown hand came to rest on her shoulder and once again, Caroline felt the unusual warmth and comfort. ''The cabin belongs to Diego, as does the land bordering mine. On occasion he leases the cabin. More often, it shelters friends in need of retreat.''

She'd ordered him around and tried to give him a tip last night, then wondered at his brusque refusal. Her cheeks burned. ''Why didn't he tell me?''

The ancient hand soothed up and down her arm. ''My grandson has his own battles to fight.''

''What kind of battles?'' As soon as she said it, Caroline knew the man she'd met wouldn't appreciate her prying.

''He almost died, but he would not let death take him.'' Sharp, proud eyes turned to hers. ''Diego was in the Special Forces.''

''Special Forces? But they're—'' Warriors, she thought. Deadly ones. She tried to picture the man she'd met as a warrior and found that she had little trouble.

''He is retired now, after a serious injury. They said he would never walk again, but my Diego has always been proud and stubborn. He proved them wrong.''

The limp. Caroline remembered now the faint limp that had seemed so out of place in the tall, striking man. She'd been too tired to notice much, but she remembered his unusual light eyes, so at odds with the black hair and sharp-bladed, copper-skinned face. "How did he get those eyes?" she mused, unaware that she'd said the words aloud.

"Diego is half-Anglo on his mother's side. It has always been a battle for both him and his brother Jesse—this feeling of being caught in two worlds.'' Then she frowned. "He helps me with my patients, but he does not yet believe in the role he will play.''

Patients? Caroline was just about to ask more, when the hoofbeats grew louder, commanding her attention.

With the previous night's exhaustion now vanquished, Caroline took a new look at him as he dismounted and tied the reins to Adelaida's fence. He stood several inches taller than her, slightly too gaunt for his big frame, deep lines carved in a face suited to a painting of Aztec warriors standing their ground against invading conquistadors. He even had the long black hair.

The only thing that didn't match was those eyes— not gray, not blue, so light they seemed to see more deeply than most. The eyes of a mage, of a sorcerer, irises banded by a dark ring, framed by heavy brows and sooty, thick lashes.

"Good morning, *m'ijito*," the old woman said. "Did you come for breakfast?"

Caroline snapped out of thoughts she could only call fanciful, totally uncharacteristic of her.

Diego met her gaze, his own scrutiny intense and unwelcome. Then he turned to his grandmother, his harsh features breaking into a smile of deep affection. "If I had, I'd be at least two hours late, wouldn't I?"

Adelaida smiled. "Another meal would not hurt you. You need more meat on your bones."

"You'd feed me until I looked like Dulcita." He grinned, turning to Caroline. "I see you and my grandmother have met already."

"She was—" Caroline gestured toward the garden. "She showed me her plants."

"Caroline is a good audience for an old woman's chattering," Adelaida said. "We are about to have tea. Would you like to join us?"

"I should go," Caroline interjected. "I need to finish my run."

"Perhaps you should not try it again so soon after losing your balance," Adelaida murmured.

The pale eyes sharpened on her. "You were running?"

She didn't like his tone. "I've run every morning for years. I know what I'm doing."

"You got light-headed, right?"

She shrugged. "After my accident, I had to stop until recently. I'll get back in shape soon." *Not that it's any of your business,* she didn't add.

"You're here from Dallas?"

She nodded.

"You've come nearly five thousand feet in altitude. Give your body a chance to acclimatize before you try running again."

"How long?" Good grief. She should have thought of that herself.

"Ease up the rest of the week. Walk instead of run, drink plenty of water and rest more often. By the weekend, your body should have adjusted, but work up to your normal running distance in stages for another few days after that."

To deny his expertise would be uncharitable. "I guess you learn about physical conditioning in the Special Forces."

His gaze shot to his grandmother's. "Someone's been talking out of school."

Adelaida only smiled serenely, placing one hand on his arm. "My Diego *es un médico.* He cared for all the members of his team."

"*Médico?* You were a medic?"

Diego nodded and looked away, a muscle in his jaw jumping.

"My grandson is a healer, just as I am."

Caroline frowned. "Are there no doctors nearby?"

Adelaida shook her head. "The nearest medical facility is one hundred thirty-five miles away."

"What sort of equipment do you have?" she asked Diego.

Adelaida answered first. "Our ways do not require medical instruments or machines."

"But how can you possibly—"

"Mama Lalita—" Diego intervened, respect and affection softening his tone. "Dr. Malone said she must go."

Adelaida's gaze took in her grandson's obvious discomfort. Shaking her head, she lifted wise eyes to Caroline. "If you will wait a moment, I will bring you the tea we discussed. Please avoid caffeine and drink it, instead." She aimed a pointed glance at Caroline's hand. "It will be a good first step on your road to healing." After a gentle pat on Caroline's shoulder, she turned toward her house.

With her went all warmth. Diego shifted his weight, and Caroline remembered his injury.

"Would you like to sit down?"

"No." He crossed his arms over his chest. Silence clogged the air around them.

"You don't have to wait with me," she said. I'm sure you're very busy—"

He didn't let her finish. "My grandmother has delivered babies, healed the sick, comforted the dying for many years before I was born. The people here respect her and love her. What she does may not conform to the training either of us received, but it works for them. They are not stupid or ignorant, only poor. She is not a quack. Whatever your opinion of the medical value of what she does,'' he said, ''I would appreciate it if you would use some restraint in letting your cynicism show. She has no bias against doctors and often refers patients when needed, but most of them cannot pay for expensive medical care. Her way is ancient and honored, no matter that you believe it to be primitive.'' His jaw flexed again. ''The scalpel, Dr. Malone, does not cure all ills.''

That stung. ''I meant no disrespect to your grandmother. I think she's a very kind and compassionate woman.''

''But?'' he challenged. ''Misguided? Ignorant of proper medical treatment?''

His anger had claws. He was a stranger, and his contempt dug deep into raw, vulnerable flesh. For a few moments, drifting in the lazy morning sun with Adelaida, she'd let her guard down. Forgotten that she belonged nowhere, that her life was a shambles. Now she had the awful, unthinkable urge to cry.

No one made Caroline Malone cry. ''No *but,* Mr. Montalvo. I'm only staying for a short while. What goes on around here is none of my business. Please tell your grandmother that I'll come back later for the tea. Tell her I suddenly felt tired or—'' Her voice wavered. Horrified, she whirled away. "I don't care what you tell her. Just—'' She shot him a glare that somehow got lost through an odd haze that blurred her vision. "Be kind. Say something kind.''

She wouldn't run away; she never ran from any confrontation. Instead, she walked through the gate and down the road, head high despite the lingering sense of shame that he'd been exactly right, and a kind, generous woman deserved more. Despite the equal urge to throw something at another man who had a need to whittle her down to size.

When she reached her cabin, she locked the door and sank against it, shocked to see her fingers tremble, to feel the shaking in her knees. The control that was second nature felt more like wallpaper stretched over a gaping hole.

Caroline gulped hard and wrapped her arms around herself. She'd never felt so alone, wishing she had someone to call, somewhere to go.

She clenched her jaw, squeezed her eyes shut. She hadn't cried once since the accident. She wouldn't start now.

But despite her resolve, the hated tears came.

CHAPTER THREE

DIEGO STARED after her. It had been a long time since he'd been this angry. He'd lived in a state of rage after the ill-fated mission; to get better, he'd had to be ruthless in paring away his explosive nature. He'd become an emotional ascetic, banishing all passions from his life but one: getting out of that damn bed.

So what had brought it back? With the ease of long practice, he took a deep, cleansing breath to release the tension that would impair his ability to look inward, to probe for the sore tooth she had jarred. Staring out over his grandmother's garden, watching Caroline Malone's slender frame recede into the distance, he let his mind wander, seeking the source of his fury.

Part of it was sheer unwelcome physical response, he knew. Edgy and too-thin and nervous as she was, she was still a beautiful woman. He didn't think she realized that. She didn't flirt; she had no come-hither stare as women often did around him, no matter that he was aware that his looks were nothing of his making, without value or meaning.

Given her profession, she would have appreciated her mind and relied on it. Would have developed the muscles of her will and determination, not practiced skills with makeup or hair or showcasing the curves of her body. He had a sense that her body was, to her, a machine accorded constant maintenance solely for it to perform at the service of her ambition—

Bingo. Ambition was the blow she'd struck that had hit home.

As a boy, Diego had lived secure in a family filled with love, never questioning his place in the world until his father had died. Even then, his mother and Mama Lalita kept him and Jesse safely grounded in the knowledge that they were cherished and special. When his mother had married Hal MacAllister and moved from the little house where they'd been surrounded by kin, Hal had settled them not far away and welcomed Roberto Montalvo's family into their lives. Diego had seen enough stepfathers since then to know just how lucky he and Jesse had been.

But their high school had drawn from many miles around, and they'd been thrown together with kids from backgrounds less understanding of diversity. Diego had learned the double-edged blade of his mixed heritage—too big and athletic to ignore when choosing teams, too Latino to bring home to lily-white parents.

Meanwhile, his mother and Hal had had three more children, solidly Anglo, free to belong where he and Jesse never would. No matter how hard they worked not to favor any of their children, Grace and Hal could not extend their protective shield to the outer world. Diego loved his stepsiblings and was still very close to them. Zane and Cade and yes, even Jenna, had gotten into more than one fight defending their elder brothers' right to be considered equal to any.

But within Diego had grown a powerful need to gain the acceptance of the wider world, to prove that he fit into the mainstream, that he could take on all comers. He worked overtime to stamp out every trace of the culture that would forever be engraved upon his features.

He wasn't proud of it, now that he'd had plenty of time to think about how he must have hurt Mama Lalita, especially, by turning his back on a place that had cradled and cherished him. Even his mother had shown her disappointment when he'd rejected the heritage she'd tried so hard to keep alive for him in respect for his father's memory.

Diego didn't even want to think how much his dad would have been wounded by him.

First in college, then in the service, Diego had made his mark, respected and admired, expected to rise high. He'd been proud to be in the Special Forces, to fight for his country and the band of brothers who only saw a man's skills and not his skin.

And then had come the mistake in Bosnia three years ago when he'd lost two men and almost died himself. Released from the hospital, Diego had traveled home for lack of anyplace better to go, sick and lost and angry. No idea what to do next, all his plans in ruins. Lashing out like a bear with a fencepost-sized thorn in his paw.

While his family closed around him and smothered him in comfort, the best Diego could manage was to brood—a far better alternative, he reasoned, than striking out at people who had nothing to do with his failures to save his men and only wanted to help him make the transition to a new life.

But he didn't want a new life. He wanted his old one back and his men safe and healthy in it.

Mama Lalita was a cagey old woman, though. She let the rest of them soothe and flutter, but aside from sending him treats, she left him alone. She didn't try any of her time-honored practices, no *pláticas* to talk out his pain, no *limpias* to sweep him clean of misery, no massage or soothing teas or baths to release the *bilis* of his rage. No ceremony to ameliorate the wounding she called *susto*.

Instead she let him get sick to death of brooding before she made her move. She would visit and ask his medical opinion about a patient or, better yet, she would send word with Jenna or Cade or Zane about some unusual problem she swore she couldn't diagnose. He'd been aggravated as hell that she wouldn't leave him alone but out of his mind from boredom. Understanding him better than anyone, she used his curiosity to lure him out of his cabin.

And then the trap was sprung. From that day, she involved him in more and more of her cases. Hampered by the crutches to which he'd graduated despite warnings he would never leave a wheelchair, Diego decided to join the land of the living and fought his way past crutches, then cane, to stand at last on his own two feet again.

Bit by bit, one wily old woman helped draw out the poison of his fury, all the while slipping him pieces of traditions that went back centuries in the blood he shared with her. Slowly he'd hit his stride feeling, if not a worthy successor to her, at least useful and productive again. He'd come to understand that what the outside world saw as metaphysical mumbo-jumbo instead was an age-old body of knowledge with a long track record of success— healing by recognizing that a patient's physical condition was intimately connected to his mental and spiritual well-being.

He thought he'd gotten comfortable with his new place in that world, no matter his doubts about Mama Lalita's assurance that he had only scratched the surface of his abilities. He was carving out his own path, mingling the best of ancient wisdom and modern medical practices.

Then into the mix had walked Dr. Caroline Malone, a living embodiment of the life he'd lost. And the look of disappointment in those green eyes unraveled three years of painstaking weaving.

She didn't believe, and she made him doubt again. Made him question if he was hiding, unwilling to reenter the game because he'd lost so spectacularly before.

He could deal with being mistaken for a caretaker and rendered invisible. He could deal with her skepticism about a different method of healing from what she knew.

But making him see himself through her eyes as someone who could have been more, churning up waters that had taken him months to still…that was something else altogether.

The sooner she left, the better.

He shook his head that he'd let her bother him. It didn't matter what she thought. She would only be here a month.

No sweat.

Now he braced for the scolding he would get from Mama Lalita when she discovered he'd run off her guest. With a quick, rueful grin, he reached for the screen door handle, readying himself to offer to deliver the tea as penance.

DRAINED BY THE STORM of tears she was ashamed of shedding, Caroline entered the kitchen on shaky legs and filled a glass with water, which she then gulped down too fast. She stared out the window at the pasture dotted with prime horseflesh, a fierce, bone-deep longing to leap on one of them and ride out this tumult alive inside her.

Finally, pride returned to steady her. With it came anger. How dared he? Who did he think he was? She'd had more medical training than he could imagine, had saved countless lives. Adelaida was kind and well-meaning, but no amount of herbs could—

It didn't matter. She'd stay out of his way and do as planned. Catch up on her reading. Tackle the needlework that would help restore the precision of her hands. Take a lot of naps, build up her strength—

And try not to go out of her ever-lovin' mind.

She glanced at the cell phone lying on the counter. She wanted to dial her office, to make contact, to touch again the life she knew. To check on her patients, though they were her partners' patients now.

As she eyed the phone with as much longing as any drunk's gaze ever caressed a bottle, a knock sounded on her door. Glancing through the glass top of it, she saw a frame too imposing to be anyone else but Diego.

The urge to hide competed with one to make clear

to him just how little standing he had to criticize her.

Instead she assumed the mask she wore when she had to deliver bad news, the one that was made of Kevlar and would let nothing past.

She pulled the door open, expecting the worst.

Instead, he greeted her with a smile. "Hello," he said, brandishing a tin in one big hand, its design a mosaic of hot orange, sunny yellow and peacock blue. "My choices were to deliver this to you with an apology or meet Mama Lalita in the woodshed."

Lines around his silvered eyes crinkled as his lips curved in a smile that must have stolen hearts all his life. Beautiful white teeth against copper skin. Dangerous, that smile was, all the more so for its contrast to his normally stoic demeanor.

Dangerous enough to make her take a step back.

"Forget it." Good grief. She'd met men more classically handsome, even dated them. She grasped for the robes of Queen Caroline but found only a tattered shred. "I don't need an apology. You're right—I don't understand your way. I don't understand how you could—" She shook her head again. "It doesn't matter. I do know people all over the world have different protocols for healing."

"But yours is better," he said.

"I didn't say that."

"You didn't have to."

"It was yours, too. Why did that change?"

"You'd have to—" Those crystalline eyes focused on her like a laser. "Come see for yourself, why don't you?"

Caroline frowned. "No. I couldn't."

"Why not?"

"Because—" She didn't know why not, just that she felt too much at sea already. She was supposed to be storing up her strength to return with a vengeance. "I have to rest."

"How many hours a day can you do nothing?" His eyes scanned the room, lighting on the bookshelves. "Ah. I got it. You're a slow reader."

She glared. "Of course I'm not."

He grinned. "You don't strike me as the kind to sit around very well."

She drew herself up. "What makes you think that?"

His gaze dipped to her feet. She realized one foot was tapping.

"Greyhounds are meant to race, not sit by the fire. You're meant to heal people, not lie around. Come with me, just once. There's an old man who needs someone with your expertise."

"I can't—" She glanced at her injured hand, slipping it beneath the other elbow.

He looked at her hand and started to speak, but didn't. "All right." He shrugged as though it wasn't important. "If you're determined to rest, my grandmother's tea will help. Let me make some for you."

Then he stepped forward as if she couldn't possibly refuse.

She moved out of his way as he strode toward her kitchen, his limp barely perceptible.

"Tell me how it happened," she said. "Your hip."

His step faltered. "Just an accident." He crossed to the cabinets and retrieved a teapot from the back of a cupboard—a gorgeous one, obviously hand-crafted, in shades of cobalt and terra cotta. Something about it reminded her of the vase. She was curious about both pieces, but more interested in hearing details of his injury, which he was obviously not going to share.

He set down the teapot. "Tell me what happened to your hand."

"I already told you. A riding accident. Is it hard for you to ride now?" Stupid question—he rode like a dream.

"Mounting and dismounting aren't so easy, but I resumed riding even before I got rid of my cane. It was the one thing I really missed while I was in the service."

"Yeah." She was silent, thinking of Star King and how she longed to be on his back.

"What about you? Afraid to ride now?" He set water to boil.

"I miss it so much some days I think I'll lose my mind, but I can't—" She looked down at her hand.

"What was the injury?"

"Humeral fracture. Radial nerve damage."

"And you're right-handed?"

She nodded.

"Tough break. How much grip strength have you gotten back?"

"Not enough." She frowned. "I can grip some, but I can't release."

He crossed the distance between them. "May I look at it? I'll be careful."

She hesitated. For too long now, touching had meant pain. In the beginning, she'd felt nothing; Don had been ecstatic when she'd regained sensation, but the odd, electrical shooting pains had worn her down. Medications didn't help. Exercise and use made them worse.

"Never mind," he said. "I shouldn't have asked."

"It's all right," she said, understanding medical curiosity. "It's just that once I started regaining sensation, all I felt was pain. The hand's better now, but—" She held it out, hating the sight of the fingers that hung like limp stalks.

"Nerves take a long time to heal." He placed her hand on top of his outstretched palm with care.

In his grip, she trembled like the frightened animal she was, tensing against the urge to snatch her hand away.

Somehow, though, Diego's touch soothed. With

extreme gentleness, he turned her hand over, stroking her thumb, softly touching the metacarpal joints beneath her fingers. His fingers supported her wrist, and warmth slid over her skin and up her arm, surprising her with the comfort of it. There was about him an element of that same peace, that slow, deep river of patience she'd felt from his grandmother, despite the other parts of him that got under her skin.

"Am I hurting you?"

"No."

"Nerve pain is tricky. It wears you down." He placed his other hand on top. "Take a slow, deep breath," he coaxed. "Nothing will harm you here."

His voice inspired trust. Conveyed strength and some darker admission of knowledge. He had known pain, too. He had had to fight to heal.

So she kept her eyes closed and simply breathed until her heart stopped racing and her legs didn't twitch with the urge to run.

The tea kettle began to whistle.

He let go carefully and crossed to the teapot, pouring some water inside, then swirling the teapot to warm it. The contrast struck her: pottery dwarfed by strong, rugged hands wrapped around it with such care. She couldn't take her eyes off the long fingers, the wide palms.

"Why are you here? Did you overdo it in therapy?"

She jerked her gaze from his hands. "How did you know?"

He glanced over, one dark eyebrow cocked. "You mean besides the fact that you have to be driven to become a cardiac surgeon, much less one so invaluable that the hospital administrator himself would look for a place for you to rest?" He grinned. "Or maybe because you're tense and exhausted and bored out of your mind after less than twenty-four hours."

"You can't know that."

He finished putting water and the herbs in the pot, then turned to her, crossing his arms over his broad chest. "But I'm right, aren't I?"

She could see in him the arrogance required for the dangerous work he'd once done. "Maybe." Then she cocked her head. "Or maybe you did the same thing. Did you push too hard in therapy, Mr. Know-It-All?"

He grinned again, and she thought there ought to be a law against any man looking like that. He tipped an imaginary hat. "Twice. Got busted both times."

For the first time since Don had refused her treatment until she took a break, Caroline could see the slightest bit of humor in what had been the most agonizing period of her life.

And so she smiled back. "I hate that they can do that."

"Yeah." There was understanding in his voice as he studied her. "But if you don't listen to the coach, you'll never get back in the game. And that's important, isn't it?"

"It's everything." When a shadow darkened his eyes, she was sorry she'd said that. He hadn't made it back into his game.

But he could be doing so much more. Why wasn't he in med school or something else where he could use his medical skills properly?

Diego busied himself pouring her a cup of tea. "Then you'd better get started on that resting. And if you get bored enough, you can make rounds with me."

Caroline accepted the cup, shaking her head. She didn't know him and would never see him again once the month ended. It wasn't her business what he chose to do. "Thanks, but I don't see the point."

His dark brows drew together. "Maybe that you could be helpful to people in need, like in that oath you swore?" His voice was harsh with challenge. "Of course, they can't pay your prices, so it would be a waste of your time, wouldn't it?"

Caroline bit back the urge to defend herself with stories of her pro bono patients. "I'm not a family physician. My skills wouldn't help."

"You went through medical school, didn't you? You had to learn the basics."

"That was a long time ago. I don't remember any of it."

He towered over her, his manner anything but calming now. "Don't want to waste your talents on the mundane, Dr. Malone? Or are you just afraid? It's like riding—you never totally forget how."

"I'm not afraid." She stood up to him, toe-to-toe, the way she'd had to do so many times before in her life. "I just don't see how I could—"

"Fine," he snapped, brushing past her to the door. "Forget I asked. Forget that an old woman who needs to rest worse than you do is still taking twenty patients a day when her back aches and her feet hurt and she gets short of breath—" He grabbed the knob and leveled a hard look at her. "And you could help, but you won't."

"You don't understand," she replied, stung. "I would if I could, but—"

"Never mind." He closed the door behind him, leaving accusation throbbing in the empty air where he'd stood.

"Without my hand, I'm useless," she finished in a strained whisper to an empty room.

And scared. So very scared.

CHAPTER FOUR

Moonlight carved thick bars across the wide plane of Diego's bed. Shoving the covers aside, he rumpled the pure geometry of light and dark. Sleep was a cruel mistress, taunting and elusive most nights, the pain in his once-shattered leg never far from the surface. Containing enough metal for a junkyard, his left side reminded Diego often that he was no longer the man who had run for miles bearing a comrade on his shoulders without breaking a serious sweat.

Sometimes it was not pain that held him from the sweet embrace of sleep; sometimes it was the faces of the men who were as much brothers as Jesse.

Except Jesse still lived. Thank God.

Scrubbing his hands over his face, sliding them back over the hair that brushed his shoulders, Diego arose. The bad leg gave way, and he gripped the headboard to steady himself.

Warm fur brushed his bare thigh in sympathy.

"Hey, boy, you want out?" Diego asked, gripping Lobo's ruff. "Just give me a minute." Jaw tight, Diego rubbed the knotted muscles and forced himself to straighten.

Lobo never moved from his side, only whimpering once. Solid black, part German shepherd and part God knows what, he cocked his head and watched Diego out of wolf-yellow eyes that seemed to see more than any dog should.

The vet had guessed that Lobo was about five years old, but something ancient stared from his eyes, perhaps formed from the pain of his past. Lobo understood pain, too, Diego knew. He'd been beaten and half starved when he'd crawled up to Diego's cabin two years ago, his fur matted with the bloody tracks of a mountain lion's claws. In a towering rage after yet another fall, Diego had just shattered a coffee mug against his fireplace when he'd heard the whimper outside. He'd had to pull himself along the floor to investigate.

Lobo and he had healed together, Lobo much faster, of course. Every step of the way—every fall, as well—Lobo had been by his side, patient and strong and watchful.

Mama Lalita called Lobo Diego's *ángel de la guarda*—his guardian angel. Though Lobo was black as pitch and fearsome looking enough to frighten children, *ángel* he was to Mama Lalita. The years of abuse had made him wary of humans, but he loved Diego's grandmother.

Diego had been forced to order Lobo not to follow him on his rounds where the dog's fear of humans battled with his need to protect his master. But he was Diego's shadow whenever allowed, always there when he sensed pain, always watching.

"Okay," Diego said, straightening. His gaze landed on the cane he kept by his bed. Tonight the support called like a lover, but he refused to yield. If he'd keep moving, the cramped muscles would eventually loosen.

He took one short step, then another. Lobo walked pressed against his weak side. On the third step, Diego's leg faltered, and he grasped Lobo's ruff for support, swearing.

Breathe deeply. Relax the leg. Picture the muscle fibers lengthening...smoothing.

It would work. Eventually it would work. Today would be a bad day, he could tell, but he would not give in to the pain. He had thought to go to his spring, to let the waters and the moonlight bathe away the memories that left him sleepless this night, but that was not an option now. Even if he could make the walk, the cold waters that so often cleansed his spirit would only tighten his tortured muscles.

"It's the whirlpool tonight for me, buddy," he said, scratching Lobo behind one ear. "You want out to run? One of us ought to be having some fun." He hobbled to his bedroom door to let Lobo go.

But Lobo padded over to the bathroom door and

stared at Diego with patient eyes. Diego realized that, once again, it wasn't Lobo's discomfort that had brought the dog to his side.

It was Diego's.

Diego eyed the distance he must cross to get to the relief the whirlpool promised. He thought of the painkillers he kept in his medicine cabinet, small sirens singing lovely, dangerous melodies of oblivion and comfort. They were at least six steps closer than the tub. Diego heard their call this night like the sighs of a seductress and wondered yet again why he didn't just throw them away, why he kept them there to tempt him.

But he knew why. Victory only came in having escape right at his fingertips and turning away from its allure.

His pain was a reminder. His men had no escape, no sighing sirens to pleasure them. They would never again feel a lover's arms, never hear birdsong, never greet the kiss of morning sun.

Diego might still have all those things, might have even more. He had plenty of years left to enjoy so much that his men had lost forever.

His pain was his penance. He would honor his men, would remember them with every halting step, every dark night without sleep.

"Come on, boy," he murmured. "Let's run that water."

Lobo walked halfway back to him, then sat as if

understanding Diego's need to stand alone. When Diego reached his side, Lobo turned and escorted him the rest of the way, a silent, sturdy guardian.

CAROLINE FLIPPED ON the light over the kitchen sink and eyed the old enameled coffeepot, wondering if she could figure out how to make a decent cup with it.

She glanced at her watch. 2:00 a.m. She'd slept the afternoon away, slept past dinner, slept more hours at one sitting than she had in years.

You have not rested well in a very long time, have you? Adelaida wasn't kidding when she'd said that tea would help Caroline sleep. She glanced at the teapot Diego had used to brew the tea for her and took one step away. If that was chamomile, it was a wonder the Victorians hadn't all been in comas.

She could brew some coffee—if she could figure out the pot—and use the quiet hours of the night to get some of her reading done.

Quiet hours. Right. All the hours were quiet here.

Caroline whirled and began to pace. What was she going to do with the time she had to fill? She wouldn't need physical therapy after a month of this; they'd be locking her up in a padded cell.

You could make rounds with me.

Diego's accusing eyes rose before her. *It's like riding. You never forget how.*

But he didn't understand. She couldn't ride and

she couldn't practice medicine. She'd lost everything that meant anything to her, all in one moment of negligence, one instant she would give everything she owned to have back, to be able to do over.

If only she hadn't relaxed. Hadn't closed her eyes to soak in the bliss that seemed light-years away now.

Caroline shook her head and started toward the coffeepot. She couldn't undo what had happened, but she could use what had served her well for years, far better than relaxing ever had. She could work, even if work now meant only reading. Sharpen the mind and the body will follow. Get back in the game one step at a time.

But when she reached the stove, making coffee seemed a waste of time, too, so she reversed her steps and grabbed as many professional journals as she could hold in one hand. She sat down on the weary green sofa, opened the first one and began to read.

When the print blurred, she blamed the lousy lighting in this back-of-beyond cabin. She kept reading until her eyes wouldn't stay open.

Just for a minute, she thought. *I'll just rest them for a minute.*

The next thing she knew, it was morning.

CAROLINE ADJUSTED the showerhead as water drummed against the sides of the old tin shower stall. *Rustic* didn't begin to describe this place, though she had to admit that everything worked and the cabin was spotless.

Washing her hair was still an adventure, but at least she had regained enough grip in her right hand to manage it herself. Accustomed to quick, efficient showers that took little time out of her busy life, she had found it excruciating to have to wait on others to help her in the months when she'd had no use of that hand. Buttons and zippers might as well have been the Himalayas for all the chance she'd had of conquering them. Simply donning clothes had been an undertaking of epic proportions.

She looked in the mirror over the ancient pedestal sink as she dried herself. Her hair, always short and razor cut for the sake of time, was shaggy now and neared her shoulders in the back, too much a symbol of the disorder of her life.

She should get it cut. *Shape up or ship out, Malone.* But where would she find a substitute for her hairdresser Gregory, here in the middle of nowhere?

Dogs barked outside and drew her notice. She saw the foal from yesterday out the window, in high spirits once again. She picked up her coffee cup and took a sip as she watched—

Gad. With a shudder, Caroline set the cup down. Maybe Adelaida could explain to her how to make coffee in that pot.

It was Diego's coffeepot, but she didn't want to talk to him.

She heard a whinny and glanced out the window. She did want to see Diego's horses, though. She poured the coffee down the sink and left the bathroom to dress.

A few minutes later, she stood out on the porch, drawing in deep breaths of crisp air, scenting all manner of aromas she didn't know but found very agreeable. Okay, so it was rustic as the devil and not her kind of place at all, but there were some good things about it.

Joyous barking greeted her as Dulcita waddled around the corner.

Caroline smiled. "Well, hello there." She descended the steps and crouched to pet the old dog. "I didn't know you could walk this far. It's good for your girlish figure, though."

Dulcita's tail wagged as she pressed her head into Caroline's hand. "Oh, aren't you a soft touch?" Caroline said.

A big, dark shape materialized around the corner and drew her attention. Huge. A wolf or— The beast growled deep in his throat.

Caroline took a step back. "Dulcita, come here. Come away. That thing might—"

But Dulcita abandoned her and headed straight for the menacing stranger.

"Dulcita," Caroline called. "Come back."

The huge beast stepped between them, and Caroline readied herself to rescue the old dog—

Dulcita nudged him, tongue panting and tail wagging as though fast friends.

"Don't hurt her—" Caroline took a step toward him.

The growling increased. Caroline halted, every nerve on edge. She looked around for something to defend herself with, something to hit him with if he hurt Dulcita—

He growled once more, then did an amazing thing.

He sat down. Placing himself between her and Dulcita as if to protect the elderly dog, the huge black beast settled on the ground, yellow eyes on alert.

"Dulcita?" Caroline called.

The old brown dog nuzzled against him, then looked over at Caroline with calm patience.

Caroline backed up the steps, then leaned against one post, staying alert in case he attacked.

But the dog—if that was what it was—merely cocked his ears high and studied her, his body language majestic, warning implied.

She had the oddest feeling that both of them thought they were protecting Adelaida's fat old dog.

A whistle pierced the air. "Lobo—" called a voice Caroline recognized only too well.

The black dog also recognized it. Ears pricked,

he rose, sparing one last glance for Caroline, as if prepared for attack.

"Lobo—" The whistle again.

The black beast, who must be Lobo, nudged Dulcita to rise and herded her out of sight around the corner. A bemused Caroline descended the steps to watch them.

She didn't have to go far.

The huge, menacing animal leaned into Diego's side, his eyes closing in rapture as Diego's hand slid into the ruff, scratching and stroking. On Diego's other side, Dulcita wagged her tail as the tall man leaned down to pet her more gently.

Caroline rounded the corner, and the black dog exploded into action, his powerful muscles surging into a leap that placed him squarely in front of Diego and Dulcita, a far deeper and more dangerous growl erupting from his throat.

Caroline froze.

"Lobo—" Diego's sharp command stopped the dog in midmotion. "Heel."

Lobo stopped, but he didn't return to Diego's side as ordered, his big body coiled with power, trembling to be set free.

"Lobo," Diego snapped. "Down."

Lobo dropped to his belly, his ruff bristling, his growl unending.

Caroline started to back up.

"No," Diego commanded. "Don't move. Stay

where you are.'' He walked toward her, crouching at Lobo's side and placing one hand in the dog's collar, talking softly to him. The dog never took his eerie yellow gaze from her, but his muscles relaxed somewhat.

"Walk over here slowly," Diego said to her.

"Are you kidding me? I'm not getting near that beast." Caroline could feel her heart pounding. "He should be locked up. He's dangerous—"

"Stop shouting. You're only making him more nervous."

"I'm not—"

Diego shot her a warning glance, and she saw the dog's muscles coil again.

Caroline lowered her voice. "He has no business running loose. I was only going to pet Dulcita, and he—"

"He was abused. He's afraid of people." Diego kept his own voice low and calm. "And he isn't running loose. He's on his own land."

Caroline glanced at the dog and saw him edging on his belly to place himself once again between her and Diego. "He's trying to protect you, isn't he?"

Diego nodded. "We've been through some hard times together. When he came to me, he was starved and filthy, covered in scars from beatings. He'd been attacked by a mountain lion and almost died from his wounds."

The animal she saw now glowed with health, his

coat shiny and dark, his frame powerful. "Is he a wolf?"

Diego smiled at that. "No one knows. He's not purebred. The vet says he's got some German shepherd in him but isn't sure what else." He let go of Lobo's collar and resumed stroking his head, looking up at her. "I can't stay down like this much longer. If you'll come closer and let him get your scent while we're together, he'll understand that you're a friend."

Caroline recalled now that Diego's gait had been slower this morning, the limp more pronounced. Crouching like that had to be tough on his hip. She wasn't eager, however, to get close to that beast. "Couldn't we just give each other wide berth?"

Diego shook his head. "It's not a good idea. I can't be around all the time, and I don't want to pen him up for the month you're here." He glanced up, and she could see the strain on his face. "Don't be afraid. I may be crippled, but I'm still stronger than he is."

Remorse set her feet moving, if slowly. "What do I do?"

"Stop being so scared of him, for one thing."

She jerked her gaze away from the beast. "Easy for you to say."

"You know horses. They pick up on your emotions. You relax, they relax. Dogs are no different. Are you afraid of them?"

She shook her head. "Only when they're giants and look as though they'd like to tear out my throat."

Diego chuckled. She wished she thought it was funny.

"Okay." She drew in a deep breath of air and looked to the sky for inspiration. "Okay." *He's a dog. Just a dog.* With slow steps, she approached him.

When she came near enough, Diego took her left hand in his and drew her down beside him, keeping his own body between her and Lobo. "Friend, Lobo," he said, his voice deep and soothing. His other hand never stopped stroking the dog's head.

The dog still quivered, but his body relaxed a bit.

"Now let him smell your hand, just as you'd do with a horse." He let her hand go and didn't force her.

"Where's an apple when I need one?" she muttered.

Diego laughed. It was only a faint laugh, low and soft, but it relaxed something inside her, too.

"Lobo's not much on apples. Now, if you'd brought him a nice rabbit…"

Caroline jerked her gaze to his, seeing genuine amusement sparkle in those unusual eyes. Laughter looked good on him, lightening the shadows that always hovered around him.

She grinned back. "Would a doggie treat do?"

Diego chuckled again, his eyes never letting hers go. "He can only be seduced if he trusts you."

For an insane instant, Caroline wondered if the same could be said of Lobo's master.

Something changed in his expression, as though he wondered, too. For a breathless moment, she stared at him, feeling something inside her stir to life.

Dulcita waddled over just then, nudging Caroline to pet her. The touch on her injured right hand yanked Caroline back to the world. She jerked the hand into her body, nearly losing her balance.

Diego steadied her. His touch on her upper arm was too much. Too real. She started to rise and saw Lobo's frame stiffen.

Diego removed his hand from her. "Hey…" he soothed. "Relax. Don't undo our progress."

She was rattled and only wanted to get away, but she could see Diego's knees settle to the ground and knew she must be taxing his weakened hip. "Okay—" She blew out another breath. "Here goes nothing."

Diego's smile was more strained now, but he never stopped stroking Lobo. "Put your hand in mine and we'll do it together." He held out his right hand.

With trepidation not solely due to the dog, she placed her left one in his. He kept his hand flattened, his touch impersonal, but she was still all too aware of him.

She leaned forward to bridge the distance, and her thigh slid against his. She could feel the outer muscle in his leg trembling with exhaustion and knew he couldn't kneel much longer. She couldn't hesitate anymore.

Lobo sniffed the back of her hand, eyes still wary, body still tensed. Diego spoke to him in Spanish, the words soft and lovely, his other hand stroking the dog.

Dulcita wriggled into the middle of them, and both Caroline and Diego laughed. The tension of the moment evaporated.

"Should I pet him?" Caroline asked.

"Do you want to?"

"No...well, yes, but—" Then she removed her hand from Diego's and extended her hand very slowly toward Lobo's head. "He's really magnificent, isn't he?"

"Yes." Diego slid his hand over hers. "Beautiful and damaged."

Together they stroked Lobo, and Caroline thought again that the master and the beast shared a resemblance in that way. There was something deeply sad about Diego, immense personal power wielded with surprising gentleness. He might be physically damaged, but he was so striking, so strong and vital. So compelling.

She slid her fingers into Lobo's ruff and felt the scar tissue beneath.

Diego's body no doubt bore the marks of his injuries, but there were other scars, as well, not visible to the naked eye.

Diego shifted, and Caroline drew her hand away, remembering his hip. "Let me help you up," she said.

His jaw clenched. "I can do it."

"Of course you can, but what's wrong with accepting help? I can tell your hip is hurting you. There's nothing to be ashamed of."

Lobo tensed as the air around them filled with Diego's pride and Caroline's challenge.

She rose, shifting her attention to the dog.

Lobo stood but didn't leave Diego's side. As if they'd done it many times before, the dog helped the man, taking some of his weight as Diego made his way to his feet, his coppery skin noticeably pale as he straightened.

For a moment he stood staring out at the distance, shifting his weight around until his damaged leg could adjust.

"You're a very stubborn man, aren't you, Diego Montalvo?"

He turned those pale seer's eyes on her then. In them she saw pain and pride and chagrin.

"Takes one to know one, Dr. Malone."

Looking at his hard jaw, she suspected he would

walk all the way back to— She realized she didn't know how far away his house was, but it was not within eyesight.

He wouldn't accept help, but he would give it; that much she already knew.

She could give him a chance to rest first. "I made the worst coffee I've ever drunk in my life. Do you have a minute to show me how to operate that ancient pot?"

Suspicion narrowed his eyes, but all he said was, "You're not supposed to be drinking coffee. My grandmother advised you—"

"I've already slept nineteen hours," she interrupted. "Surely your grandmother is merciful enough to allow me one decent cup of coffee in the morning." She cocked her head and smiled. "You're not going to make me beg, are you?"

He studied her, and she had the sense she hadn't fooled him. After a long moment, he nodded. "All right." Then a quick grin chased over his mouth. "City slicker."

"Cowboy," she teased back, with a cheer she hadn't felt in a very long time.

CHAPTER FIVE

DIEGO CURSED in silence as he ascended the porch steps. Only three, but they might as well have been mountains. He'd been foolish to walk all the way to her cabin this morning after one of his bad nights.

His grandmother would have told him to return to bed following the soak in the whirlpool, he knew, but she made no such allowances for herself. He'd hoped to carve out a few hours before nightfall to continue repairs on the burned-out house in the village he intended to make into a clinic, but his late start made that unlikely.

He didn't have time to be teaching Caroline to make coffee.

Dr. Malone, he corrected. To think of her that way was safer. To remind himself that no matter her current fragility, she came from another world, one where he no longer fit. One where he likely never had fit, except in his own mind.

"It's wonderful!" she exclaimed over her cup of coffee. "Strong enough to melt the spoon, but I like it that way."

"But not good for you," he lectured. "You should be relaxing and letting your body heal, not jazzing it up with caffeine."

Rebellion flared in Caroline's green eyes. She sank back against the counter. "I'm sick of people telling me what I need to do."

"Can't stand not being the one in charge," he observed. "Too used to having godlike powers?"

"Don't say that," she snapped.

"Say what?" The flip from rebellion to fury intrigued him.

"I don't think I have godlike powers," she said.

"Oh, really? Then how did you get to be a surgeon? Don't you have to swear a blood oath? Comes right after the Hippocratic oath—'first, do no harm,' then 'I know all, see all—'"

She slammed her mug down, then caught his grin. "Oh—you're joking. Sorry." Her fair skin bloomed rose red.

He chuckled, enjoying the advantage. "Sore spot, Dr. Malone?"

"No." She shook her head. "Yeah. You sound too much like a fellow surgeon who thinks he's God's gift to both medicine and womankind—"

"A man who has to put a woman down isn't much of a man," he said. "Put a move on you and you didn't bite, right?"

Her eyes warmed. "I don't go for insufferable jerks."

He let the question shimmer unspoken for endless seconds while they watched each other with too many other questions crowding the otherwise quiet room.

There was no reason to ask. He did anyway. "So what type do you go for?" As soon as he'd said the words, he willed them back.

But too late. She studied him for a long time, her shoulders curving inward, her face at once very young and very old. "I...don't know," she admitted. "I haven't been—I don't have much time—" She picked up her mug and took a long sip.

In that moment, Diego saw another woman inside the tough shell of the ambitious surgeon, the woman so driven to compete that a brilliant colleague felt compelled to knock her down.

She wasn't as sure of herself as she portrayed, not so hard as she'd like to convey. Diego began to wonder if there wasn't more to it than her recent injury.

Susto. What had this woman lost of her soul? And why? All at once, Diego wished he had his grand-mother's insight.

But Caroline Malone would never stand for a healing. She would not welcome the long talks of the *plática,* the counseling where a *curandera* began to understand the pain beneath the body's illness. He tried to imagine her lying still for the cleansing *limpia—*

All at once, an image snared him: that long, slender body bared, the ivory skin softening beneath his touch as he massaged her to open her heart, readying her to accept the sweeping away of soul pain—

Cristo— Diego whirled. Unacceptable. A healer never got involved with his patient. Caroline Malone might not consider herself his patient, but she needed help.

No. From his grandmother, maybe; not from him. Not when he was so aware of her as a woman.

"What's wrong?" she asked.

"Nothing—" He barely curbed the urge to snap. "I have to go." He hadn't been involved with a woman since his injury. Now was a hell of a time for his body to be awakening.

"Is it your hip?"

"I don't need your help—" He turned back to her. "You're the patient, remember?"

Lines formed between her brows. "I'm not a patient—certainly not your patient."

"Good." He heard Lobo growl and crossed to the door. "I'm late. You should rest." He jerked the knob.

"Don't tell me what to do—"

"Fine—" he snarled.

"Just go—"

"Gladly." He slammed the door. He was halfway down the steps before it registered that there had been tears in her eyes.

Lobo's voice rumbled.

Diego swore. For a moment he considered going back to apologize.

The lock clicked into place behind him.

He looked at Lobo. "What the hell just happened, buddy?"

Lobo only whined and stood at the bottom of the steps, waiting with patient eyes.

Diego started toward his grandmother's house and the peace that always lay in wait there.

No. She would want to know what had happened. Why, for the second day in a row, he had lost a temper that he'd kept under iron control for a long time now.

He didn't know, and he didn't want to talk about it.

So though his grandmother's house was much closer and his hip hurt like hell, Diego headed, instead, up the long path that would lead to his house.

Knowing also that for the second time in as many days, he owed the prickly Dr. Malone an apology.

CAROLINE WATCHED his torturous climb back to the ridge behind her cabin. He shouldn't be pushing that hip so hard—she knew it; so did he. Damn male pride, anyway.

If she had a car, she could…

She slapped the palm of her left hand on the counter. Trapped. She was trapped here in Nowheresville with a hermit and a crazy old lady who—

Not fair, Caroline. Not even a little fair. Adelaida was as kind a soul as she'd ever met. The real Mc-Coy, someone who gave of herself to others without any hope of recompense. Just the thought of Adelaida settled her.

She eyed the cell phone. Walked halfway to it, reached to pick it up—

What would be the use? They'd say what they always said—that everything was under control, that she should just relax and get well...

Relax. Caroline snorted. How could you relax when you were going bonkers?

You could make rounds with me.

No. It was crazy. What did she remember of basic medicine? It had been years. She might do harm, forgetting something important—

An old woman who should be retired still seeing twenty patients a day—

A load for anyone half Adelaida's age. But how could she accompany Diego anywhere? He was too—

She shivered. Too big. Too overpowering. Too—

Damaged. Not his body; that didn't bother her. But within him something was still wounded. She didn't need that, didn't need anyone else's problems on top of her own.

She studied the hand that she could barely stand

to look at anymore. The contrast hurt. Once it had been a thing of grace, a tool of rare skill. Once she had taken it for granted.

No more. It was ugly and she hated it, hated what it represented to her.

Failure. Who was she, if not the miracle worker? If not Dr. Caroline Malone, possessor of multiple awards and certifications, author of important papers, admired and sought after—

If she wasn't a doctor, who was she?

Oh, God—

Left hand pressed to her mouth, Caroline removed her right hand from her blurring field of vision. She had to get out of here. Had to make something happen. She would go crazy if she didn't find—

What? She was halfway to the road before she knew it. What did she expect to find? Where was there help?

And who would care, anyway? Who would understand that she was once again the terrified teenager on the streets alone that first night with no idea where to seek shelter?

She'd stayed in the bus station all night, hiding in the rest room when the traffic thinned, scared to death that they'd throw her out on streets that seemed meaner, dirtier…but she'd known she couldn't go back. They wouldn't take her back.

Nowhere to go.

In the middle of the road, Caroline snapped from memory to present time.

It was the same now. She looked, just once, into the maw of her terror, afraid, deep inside her, that all she'd done, all she'd become, was over now and she had no future.

Nowhere to go. No one who cared.

Alone. Always so alone.

When Adelaida stepped out into the road, Caroline gasped, sure she'd imagined her.

But no. Adelaida held out a hand. "Come, child. It is a beautiful morning, and I was hoping to see you."

The welcome in that lined brown face slid into Caroline's raw heart and sent terror skittering away on unsteady legs. "I—" She couldn't figure out what to say, heart still juking and jiving out of control. "Adelaida, I—" She grasped for a safe place, an island in the middle of the sea that had been tossing her for months like so much flotsam.

One small hand reached out and clasped hers, the ugly one, the damaged one. Caroline tensed, but Adelaida wouldn't release her.

And peace slid into her the way her mother's hot chocolate had once warmed her to the core so many years ago.

"Oh, Adelaida—" Tears again. She never cried.

An arm slid around her waist, steadying her. "I know, child. I know."

And somehow Caroline thought it might really be true. Like the child she hadn't been since long before adolescence, she let Adelaida lead her into the garden.

IT WORKED. Again, it worked…Adelaida's garden refreshed like an oasis, silent and still to city ears, yet not silent at all. Humming and buzzing, bees flitted from roses to zinnias; a mockingbird warbled from a nearby tree. Beside Caroline, a small tortoiseshell cat purred.

And on her other side, Dulcita had plopped and now snored softly, the other half of an unmatched pair of bookends, unlikely guardians whose warm animal comfort settled something ragged inside Caroline.

A pet. Why had she never had a pet? When she got home, maybe she'd—

Home. Viewed from the other side of the fault line that had sundered her life, Caroline knew a moment of intense fear that she would never find a road back.

Dulcita stirred and whined.

The tortoiseshell cat arched and rubbed Caroline's leg where she knelt in the dirt.

Caroline swallowed back dread. *Don't think. Just don't think. Not yet.*

She rose, brushing dirt from her jeans. "Adelaida—''

Motion out of the corner of her eye choked off her words. A figure stood at the gate, a man with his hat in his hand. Adelaida started toward him, squeezing Caroline's arm as she passed.

"*La señora*," he began, rotating his straw hat hand to hand. He drew a young girl from behind him. A quick exchange in Spanish ensued.

The girl was pale and strained. Adelaida placed one hand on the girl's forehead, closing her eyes as the flat of her palm rested against the girl's skin. She spoke too quietly for Caroline to hear; the man's eyes closed tightly, as well.

Then she stepped back and gestured them toward her front door, pausing to look at Caroline. "Please come inside, *niña*. The sun is getting too warm."

Caroline hesitated.

Adelaida spoke. "I would appreciate it if you would cut me several stalks of *romero* about this long—" She indicated the length with her hands. "Cut it with these scissors and carry it upside down." She pulled scissors from her apron pocket. "If you are not uncomfortable helping me."

Caroline was, but she could not be so churlish as to refuse to help this woman who'd been so kind to her. She took the scissors and gathered the *romero*— rosemary in Spanish, she remembered.

The cuts weren't smooth and she'd had to use both hands on the scissors, but she'd managed. Carrying the stalks as instructed, she entered the house, not sure where they might be and concerned about interrupting.

It was her first time inside Adelaida's house. Like the outside, it bore evidence of much care and love. The furnishings, like those in her cabin, carried the weight of years. A potbellied stove stood in one corner; plants lined the windowsills. One wall was crowded with pictures Caroline itched to peruse.

As she crossed to the door from which she could hear voices, she halted in her tracks. On the old scarred dining table stood a vase filled with flowers—a vase as stunning and powerful as the one on her kitchen table. The same artisan had surely created both. This one was big and round, glazed in deep carmine red easing into a golden orange as vivid as any marigold.

And on the wall behind the table hung a painting of a couple who had to be Adelaida and her beloved Diego, rendered by an artist whose hands were surely guided by love. There was such tenderness and joy in that painting that Caroline wanted to forget her errand and simply drink in the devotion that shouted from every stroke.

"¿Niña?" Adelaida called.

Caroline jerked her gaze away from both vase and painting, resolving to find out who did them. A shared energy made her wonder if the same person had done both. Either way, she wanted to see more. Needed to see more.

Adelaida stood in a small room with few furnishings. A bed covered with clean white linen was situated in front of the window, tables on each side of it with a lamp and assorted candles on each. A chest in deep blue ornamented with tiny bright-hued flowers stood against the wall to the left, and on the wall opposite the bed, a small altar reposed. A straight-backed chair stood by the door.

The girl lay on the bed, and Adelaida spread out the girl's arms from her sides as she murmured a low, soothing chant. The father watched from the foot of the bed, just far enough back that he would not impede Adelaida as she walked around it.

Adelaida made the sign of the cross on the girl's forehead, pausing at each table to light a blue candle. She crossed to the altar and lit two more, both blue.

Caroline wondered if she should leave, but she hesitated to disturb the concentration that hushed the room.

Adelaida took an egg from one table and walked around the girl, holding the egg in her left hand just above the girl's body, sweeping over the girl from head to foot, then hand to hand in the sign of the cross, all the while speaking softly in Spanish. Then she swept from the girl's heart outward to the end of each limb.

The silent man repeated the sign of the cross as Adelaida completed each sweep of his daughter. At the finish, she bowed her head, obviously praying. Then she walked to one table, cracked the egg into a bowl and studied it as long seconds passed. From a small handmade broom propped against the wall, she took two broomstraws, crossed them and placed them in the bowl.

With a nod that seemed satisfied, Adelaida turned to the girl again, holding her hand and speaking to her in rapid-fire Spanish, occasionally touching the girl's heart or her forehead. Still holding the girl's hand, she turned to the father and spoke with him. The man nodded his understanding, then Adelaida turned to Caroline.

"Bring me the *romero,* please." After taking it from Caroline, she stepped to the altar and held the stalks on her outstretched hands, murmuring a prayer to the saint on the altar, then crossing herself again. She selected a red ribbon and tied it around the stalks, then said another prayer.

Returning to the bed, she repeated the sweeping motions with the bundle as though it were a broom, beginning at the girl's head and working down to the heart, where she paused to make the cross again. Then she worked outward from the heart once more.

The girl, whose complexion had been almost gray when she'd arrived, had regained color in her cheeks. She lay quietly, her breathing slow and deep, eyes still closed.

Then Adelaida motioned to the father to approach

the bed. He knelt by his daughter's side, and Adelaida placed his right hand over his daughter's, then put both over the girl's heart. She rested one of her hands atop each of their heads, closed her eyes and prayed.

And despite everything Caroline knew to be possible or logical, she felt the breath of sanctuary in this small, plain room.

Something deep within her stirred even as she backed away, too aware that she was a stranger who didn't belong here. Who didn't understand what she'd seen and wasn't sure she wanted to know. She cared for Adelaida, was grateful for her kindness— but this was too much. She left the room.

But before she could make her escape, the young girl emerged, eyes glowing, the picture of health. She hugged Adelaida, then Caroline, who froze like a deer in a car's beam.

"*Gracias,*" the girl said. "I am Consuela Garza and this is my father. Thank you for your help."

"I didn't—"

Consuela smiled. "*La señora* has cared for my family since my grandparents' time, but it is harder on her these days. Perhaps with you and Diego to help her, it won't be so tiring."

"I don't—I'm not—" But the girl had turned away.

Adelaida and the father conversed in Spanish. She

gave him the bowl in which she'd placed the egg. Then she gestured toward Caroline with a smile.

The father approached. "*Doctora,* I am Arturo Garza. On behalf of my child and myself, I thank you."

"But I didn't—"

Adelaida stayed her with the touch of one hand. "Dr. Malone is here only to rest and observe."

The man nodded graciously. "I would be pleased to bring you a fine hen when I bring one to *la señora.*"

Caroline opened her mouth to dissuade him, but Adelaida beat her to it. "Thank you, Arturo. As always, your fine hens will be welcome."

When they left, Adelaida gestured toward Caroline. "This must seem strange to you. Let me make a pot of tea, and I will answer any questions you might have."

Curiosity battled scorn. Caroline didn't know where to begin or if she even wanted to know. She didn't believe in whatever this was, but there was a goodness in Adelaida she could not discount.

As they passed the table, she seized on a diversion. "There's a vase in my cabin that must have been thrown by the same potter as this one. Who made them?"

Adelaida turned. "Do you like them?"

"Of course. They're stunning. Beautiful and so powerful."

Adelaida smiled. "Diego made them."

Caroline's head swiveled. "Your husband Diego?"

The old woman chuckled. "My grandson Diego."

"Diego?" she echoed. Soldier, artisan, healer—"The teapot, too?" All at once she remembered watching those long fingers cradle the teapot.

Adelaida nodded. "Yes. And in my kitchen I have mugs he made as well as two bowls."

"He's very good, isn't he?"

Dark eyes glowed with pride. "He is talented at many things, as is his brother." Adelaida pointed to the painting.

So...not the same artist but the same blood. "I wondered. There is such feeling in it. There's a power in the work of both—" She turned from her study. "What's his name?"

"Jesse. He is two years younger than Diego. They share a special bond."

"How old is Diego?"

"Thirty-eight."

"Does Jesse live around here?"

Sorrow darkened the old woman's eyes. "No. Jesse has been gone many years."

Caroline touched her shoulder. "I'm sorry." She wanted to know more but wouldn't ask.

"There are no hard feelings. Jesse is aware that he is welcome at any time. He is a busy man and he, like Diego, once thought to leave the valley for good."

"Now Diego is back." But it took injury to bring him.

"We missed him, all of us. His mother, especially."

"His mother lives around here?"

"She and his stepfather live in Alpine, about fifty miles away. He has two half brothers and a half sister, all grown."

"Where are they?"

Adelaida shrugged. "Too far. We lose our children from the valley now. The world woos them from us. Zane is an actor in California. Zane MacAllister."

"Zane MacAllister is Diego's younger brother?"

"You have seen his pictures?"

"Yes." Even busy surgeons went to the movies. Zane was hot, his star on the rise. "What of his other brother?"

"Cade is a photographer. He travels all the time. And Jenna." Adelaida's smile was sweet. "Our little Jenna is in college now."

"But she's not your—" She'd said *our.*

"It does not matter that the three youngest do not share my blood. We are family, all of us. When Roberto died, Diego's mother, Grace, was still a member of my family. And when she married Hal, he became my new son." The old woman looked deep into Caroline's eyes. "Diego has ghosts to battle, but he need not fight them alone. He is stubborn and proud, but he is much loved." A smile crinkled her eyes. "Jenna wanted to leave college to nurse him, despite the fact that her skin turns a peculiar shade of green at the first sight of blood."

"Nursing isn't easy." But Caroline's mind was on Adelaida's earlier words. What would it be like to have so many people willing to fight for you? Devoted to loving you?

"Come, *niña*." Adelaida touched her arm. "Let me make you tea."

She wanted to—oh, how she wanted to sink into the comfort of this place and this woman. To pretend for a while that she was part of something, that she could be so cherished and loved.

But it wasn't true. Would never be true unless she—

She had two sisters. Chloe might have changed beyond recognition, but Ivy would care. She would.

Please, Ivy. You do still care, don't you?

But if she didn't—

"I'm sorry, Adelaida. I need to—" Caroline turned away, then back, grasping the older woman's hand. "Thank you. I want to stay, but I—" Those brown eyes looked upon her with such kindness that Caroline almost relented. Almost threw herself into this wise old woman's arms and held on.

But too much had happened this morning.

You made mistakes when you didn't think things through carefully. Caroline couldn't handle any more mistakes just now.

"Sh-h," Adelaida soothed, squeezing her hand, patting her arm. "I will be here when you are ready."

Caroline could only nod as she hunched her shoulders against the ache inside her chest. "Thank you," she murmured, walking away from what she wanted to grab with both hands.

She reached the door just as Diego stepped inside.

He got a good look at her and frowned. "What's wrong?"

With a muffled cry, she brushed past him and ran.

CHAPTER SIX

DIEGO WATCHED HER GO, her gait awkward and uneven. He turned to his grandmother. "What happened?"

"Pobrecita," his grandmother said, shaking her head. "Poor little thing. There is such pain in that one, such need for love."

He didn't want to feel impatience with Mama Lalita. "Tell me what's going on."

Wise old eyes lifted to meet his. "I am not sure. Arturo Garza brought Consuela for another *limpia.* Caroline was here—"

He would have expected a different reaction. She should have been sneering, not devastated. The woman he'd glimpsed as she'd raced past had not been the brilliant surgeon, looking down her nose at primitive rituals.

She'd been fragile as a moth's wing. Easy to crush.

"I have to go to her." Even as he said it, Diego saw the folly of it. He had no business getting involved. She would be gone in a matter of short weeks. There were deep rifts within Caroline Malone, far deeper than she would allow anyone to see, much less heal.

But he was a healer. Not the best one, not of his grandmother's stature—

Reasoning out why he must go to her was useless. It simply was.

He turned from staring out the door to tell his grandmother he was leaving—

She stood there with a solemn half smile. "I fear for your heart, *m'ijo,* but it is you she needs."

He looked at his grandmother helplessly. "I should stay far away from her. This makes no sense."

"Destiny seldom does."

"Mama Lalita—" he warned. "You know I don't believe in that."

Her smile widened. "Go then. Prove me wrong."

His own lips quirked. "You make me crazy, *Abuela.*"

Her eyes twinkled. "Yes, I know."

Diego shot her a grin and left.

When he pulled out of her drive, he aimed the pickup toward Caroline's cabin, but a glance in the rearview mirror had him turning around. The faint figure with the bright blond hair was headed in the direction of La Paloma, the tiny village that was only a cluster of less than two dozen buildings.

He pulled his old workhorse pickup even with her.

She spared him only one glance before increasing her pace, looking straight ahead like a soldier marching to battle.

"Good morning," he said.

Caroline didn't respond.

"Heading for the village?" he asked through the open window.

No answer.

"Want a ride?"

One quick shake of the head.

Temper only she could provoke raced like mercury to the danger point. Diego shoved the gearshift into Park, shut off the engine and charged out the door.

Reaching her side in only a few long strides, he grabbed her arm and whirled her toward him. Angry words died as he got a good look at her face—a thin crust of ice ready to fracture. "Caroline—" he said, gentling his touch. "Tell me what's wrong."

She blinked with the rapid beat of hummingbird wings. "Nothing. I'm fine." She wouldn't meet his eyes, drawing her arms into her body as if his touch repelled her.

Or as if kindness would shatter her.

Diego took a mental step back. A deep breath to gain needed distance. In the silence, he heard a calf bawling for his mother, a mockingbird serenading.

He dropped his hand from her arm, remembering how it was with Molly, the mare who'd been beaten and starved. Molly had bitten and kicked him, had fought him every step. He'd had to approach her time and time again, each day needing to renew his faith that he would ever reach her.

"I was on my way to town. Would you like a ride?" He kept his tone as polite as he would with a stranger.

She shook her head. "I don't—"

He held his hands out, palms outward. "Just a ride, Caroline. That's all I'm offering."

She measured him out of the corner of one eye. "All right, but I'll walk back by myself."

He shrugged. "Fine. I'll be there for a while, anyway."

Wary eyes studied him. "I'm not a charity case, Diego. Stop trying to diagnose me."

He wanted to tell her how wrong she was. Not a charity case but certainly someone in dire need of healing. "Fine. You're the doctor," he said.

She snorted. "Yeah." She walked past him to the passenger side of a pickup that had seen better days.

He tamped down the urge to open the door for her, watching her try it with her right and finally resort to using both hands, her chin jutting forward as if daring him to comment.

Diego remembered only too well what it felt like

to need help and slap it away, so he merely rounded the front of the pickup and got inside.

"THERE'S REALLY A TOWN ahead?" Caroline heard rust in her voice, as if the minutes passed in complete silence had dried it up.

Diego glanced at her. "You didn't see La Paloma on your way to the cabin?"

"I thought maybe—" She saw a cluster of buildings ahead. "I was too consumed by fury over being exiled."

A grin flared at her confession. "Well, it's not much of a town. I think people had hopes fifty years or so ago that it would grow, but there's nothing here to make that happen."

"El Paso's the closest city, right?"

Amusement threaded his tone. "You could count Juarez, I guess, but most Anglos don't."

She remembered the shacks on the other side of the interstate, the brown haze smothering them. "I've only been across the border once."

"Where?"

"Laredo."

"What did you think?"

"I—" She didn't want to admit that she never wanted to go back, that the poverty and dirt had horrified her. "It was all right."

"We're a poor people, Dr. Malone, but our lives

are not what you see on the border. Don't judge from what you witnessed there.''

''I didn't mean—''

''Yes, you did.'' He turned toward her, his jaw hard but his eyes less so. ''And I understand. I know your world.''

''It's your world, too,'' she protested. ''Adelaida told me your mother is Anglo.''

He shook his head. ''It's not my world. It never was.''

''But—''

Just then he stopped in front of a one-story wooden building with a wide front porch. Both needed paint. ''Ramón Vargas runs a small market, if you'd prefer to pick up something besides what I stocked.'' He glanced at her. ''I had no idea what you would like.''

She wanted to understand him, wanted to hear about his family from him, not his grandmother. The look in his eyes made it abundantly clear he had no intention of obliging her.

''You did all right,'' she relented. ''I would kill for fresh vegetables, though.''

''Those,'' he said, sliding from the seat, ''you can't buy here.''

She could see vegetables through the window. ''I see them inside.''

He turned and laid his arms over the open pickup window. ''Mama Lalita has vegetables to spare and it would be a mortal insult not to let her share them."

"But I can't ask her—"

"I can." He smiled, and she wondered if she'd ever quit reacting to the shock of it. "And you can bet I will."

"I'll pay her for them."

He rolled his eyes. "I don't think I've seen my grandmother angry a handful of times in my life, but I assure you that merely offering to pay her would make Pompeii look like a puff of steam."

"But, Diego—"

"I know you don't understand, but it's our way here. We share what we have—it doesn't matter that your hospital has paid for the cabin, but if it makes you feel better, consider vegetables included in the price." He held up a hand when she would have protested again. "I know—it's not her cabin, it's mine, but if you must reduce it to Anglo debts, consider that you've worked in her garden and this can be your pay." Then he eyed her and she couldn't dismiss thinking that pity lurked somewhere in his glance. "Not all the world is about checks and balances or about independence. We all need others, Caroline." He shoved away from the window. "Even you."

She wanted to argue with him, but he'd already walked into the store. She thought about staying where she was, but a flash of color in the window caught her eye. On the far side of the wooden porch sat a rocking chair. On one corner of it she saw a hat she might use to shade her from the sun.

She didn't know if it was for sale and she had no money with her to purchase anything, anyway. Now that she knew the village was less than five miles away, though, she could come back. With only a moment's fumbling, she opened the pickup door and emerged.

Just past the rocking chair, inside the window, she saw a little sign that said *Tesoros.* Next to it hung a quilt in a bold design of bright green, fiery red, ocean-deep blue. In the center glowed a sun in every shade of gold from pale lemon to hot orange. Caroline's fingers itched to touch it, as though it would thaw the frozen emptiness inside her chest.

She followed Diego's path and opened the screen door to step inside. Her gaze fastened on the quilt, and it took a minute for the explosion of aromas to register. She stopped in her tracks and looked around.

She'd never seen a grocery like this. Bare wooden floors swept painfully clean; sturdy wooden shelves shoulder-high, bearing jars and bottles and boxes she'd never seen, side by side with familiar brands. *Ristras* of red peppers and *piñatas* hung above the shelves. One shelf near her held candles bearing the likenesses of saints.

An old-fashioned ornate metal cash register stood

on the counter to her left, the wood gleaming, smelling of beeswax and lemon. To her right were grouped four tables with unmatched chairs, the tables bright with cloth she'd swear was hand-woven. Past them a woman worked in a small kitchen from which heavenly smells emerged.

Caroline's stomach growled, and she remembered that she'd been too upset to eat breakfast. Like a starving pilgrim, she took a step toward the food before recalling her lack of money.

Then she realized all talking had ceased. Only the sound of Spanish music remained. She glanced around to see every eye in the place on her. She couldn't spot Diego anywhere. She readied herself to leave.

"*¡Hola!* You must be Diego's doctor." The voice came from the kitchen. The woman who'd been cooking had turned around, greeting her with a big smile.

"Where is he?"

With a toss of black curls, she indicated the back of the store. "Talking to my brother Ramón." The woman approached, her apron a starburst of tropical birds and vivid flowers. She was a few inches shorter than Caroline's five-foot-six, curvy and gorgeous, her brown eyes friendly. "I'm Elena Vargas." She put out her hand to shake.

Caroline extended her left hand. "I'm sorry—my hand—"

Elena waved it off. *"No es importante,"* she said. "You have another one."

Before Caroline could respond, Elena had already moved on. "You look hungry. I was just working on lunch. You can be my taster."

"No, I can't—I don't have—" Caroline fumbled for minute. "I don't have any money with me."

"Pah—" With a flick of her hand, Elena dismissed Caroline's concern. "I don't charge for tasting."

Caroline frowned. "I don't need charity." Saying it underscored just how different her life was now. Once she had needed it desperately, though she'd been too proud to accept any. Her finances were now secure, but in an instant she'd reverted to the teenage runaway who understood hunger.

"I wasn't offering it," Elena responded. "But if it bothers you, we can put it on Diego's tab—" She smiled as she saw the refusal rise to Caroline's lips. "Or you can start your own."

"You don't know me," Caroline insisted. "I might not pay you."

Elena shrugged one pretty shoulder. "Of course you will. Mama Lalita wouldn't trust you if you did not deserve it."

Mama Lalita? "Is she your grandmother, too?"

Elena laughed. *"Pero,* no—but she might as well be. I spent my childhood trailing in and out of her house." She grinned. "Diego's brothers thought I was a pest, a necessary evil because Ramón had to watch me. Diego himself didn't even deign to notice that I existed.''

''Are you and Diego—?'' She broke off in mid-sentence, astonished that she would ask something so personal of someone she'd just met.

Elena laughed. ''Ah, that one—*qué padre,* eh? What a man.'' Her voice held almost a purr. ''But no, to Diego I'm no different from Jenna.'' Laughter rippled through her again. ''Except that I'm not so hardheaded.''

''Depends on who's making the call,'' said Diego from behind Caroline. ''Jenna would say she's easy-going.''

Elena laughed, and Diego chuckled along with her.

Caroline stiffened, horrified to have been caught gossiping about him. She had no interest in his personal life. None at all. ''I—uh, I was—I just came inside to look at the quilt.'' She moved in that direction.

''Ah, a woman with a taste for color,'' Elena said. *''Mi madre y mi abuela* pieced that one.''

Vibrant color had never been part of her image. Her apartment was shades of white and cream and taupe, tasteful and…

Lifeless.

Where had that come from? Her life was about order and precision, control and moderation. The pressures of her profession required them or she'd drown in the drama of life and death.

But she wanted this quilt. Somehow it called to her. "Is it for sale?"

Elena laughed. "Everything in this place is for sale. I'd sell Ramón to the right buyer."

"Not if I get a chance to sell you first," said a man's voice.

Caroline turned to see a man near Diego's age put Elena in a feigned headlock. He was several inches shorter than Diego, bulky and more rounded where Diego was tall and lean. His brown eyes sparkled as brightly as his sister's.

"Unfortunately, it doesn't take anyone long to realize that acquiring my sister would be a big mistake—" He grunted as Elena's elbow landed in his middle. "What did I tell you? I think we must auction her off, sight unseen, if we are ever to get rid of her. No man is going to put up with her mouthy ways."

"I'm not going to spoil any man the way Mariela does you. The poor woman can barely draw a breath between babies and she's still looking at you like you hung the moon. One of these days, *hermano*," Elena threatened, a smile playing around her mouth, "I'm going to take her aside and explain how that keeps happening."

"Oh, she knows." Ramón shrugged. "I can't

help it that I'm irresistible." He waggled his eyebrows, and Diego chuckled.

Elena rolled her eyes. "Careful you don't trip over that *machismo*." She swatted her brother's arm. "Come look at my *tesoros*," she said to Caroline. Tongue in cheek, she rubbed her hands. "Doctors make a lot of money, don't they? Let's see what else I can sell you."

Caroline couldn't help but laugh. "Why not? I don't even have a car to drive. I'm a captive audience."

Elena leaned over whispering like a conspirator. "If you're very generous, lunch is on me."

CAROLINE WAS GENEROUS.

In addition to the hat and the quilt, she bought an embroidered top unlike anything she'd ever worn. With Ivy so recently on her mind, she bought an apron not quite so flamboyant as Elena's and hoped that Ivy still loved to cook. It seemed a good luck charm; maybe possessing a gift for Ivy would mean Caroline would indeed find her.

She almost bought a beautiful handmade rag doll for Chloe before reality slapped her with the knowledge that Chloe would now be in her twenties.

By the time she'd gathered up all her booty, she was truly starving. She fell upon Elena's offered meal like a shipwrecked sailor come to shore. A full order of cheese enchiladas with *borracho* beans and homemade *tortillas* preceded the *sopapilla*—her third—dripping with honey and almost too hot to handle. She'd consumed a week's worth of fat in one sitting, but she couldn't recall ever enjoying a meal more.

Finally, she looked around, realizing the crowd had thinned out, and wondered where Diego had gone. It wasn't really her business; she wasn't sure how she'd transport all her goodies, but she'd told Diego she intended to walk back. She'd have to figure it out.

A glance out the front window, though, showed his pickup still parked in front. Elena returned from her kitchen area, her hair curling more tightly from the kitchen heat. "Whew—busy lunch crowd." She sank to the chair beside Caroline, slipped off her shoes and rubbed one foot.

"Where do all these people come from?" Caroline asked.

Elena shrugged. "The highway patrolmen and sheriff's deputies often stop by for breakfast or lunch. Local ranchers, people in town for groceries. A few travelers, though there aren't many who come down this road."

"Diego's truck is still outside. Do you know where he is?"

"Probably in the back, seeing patients. Either that or at the new clinic."

Patients? "He has a clinic?"

"Not a real one, no. Ramón and I cleared out a space in the back here so he could set up some equipment to do other things besides what Mama Lalita can handle and to see other people—Anglos who don't want a *curandera* but don't have the money to go to the doctor in Fort Stockton. It's not much space, though, so he's rehabbing an old house that burned and wants to turn it into a full-fledged clinic."

You could make rounds with me. "So he sees people here now instead of making house calls?"

Elena shook her head. "Oh, no. Diego still travels all over to see people who need him." She nodded toward the outside. "That old truck's got a lot of miles on it. He and Ramón keep it going, but personally, I think they need to shoot it and put it out of its misery."

Caroline didn't want to be curious, but it didn't seem to matter. "What kind of equipment does he have?"

"Not much. Not what he wishes he could get, but he's proven to be quite the scavenger, our Diego."

"Do people pay him?"

She shrugged. "Like they do Mama Lalita. Chickens and eggs, milk from a cow. Some of them trade with work, helping him tear out the burned wood on the clinic. One of the ranchers came up with some lumber, but mostly that's where Diego's savings and disability go. That and what he gets from renting the cabin.''

Caroline tried to picture Judd Carter taking a chicken in trade or driving an old pickup instead of his Jaguar.

She didn't want to see this nobility in Diego, didn't want reasons to find him more attractive than she already did.

Didn't want to feel ashamed of herself for refusing to help him.

Just then the front door opened, and Elena's eyes flared with welcome. Caroline turned to see a heavily pregnant woman walk in with an older man beside her.

"¿Mariela, cuándo va a dar a luz?" a man at a table beside them asked.

So this was Ramón's wife.

Mariela's mouth twisted in a wry grin. "Going to be in the dark for a little while yet."

Caroline glanced at Elena for translation. Having lived in Texas all her life, she recognized the words *cuándo*—when—and *luz*—light—but the rest of the phrase meant nothing.

Elena smiled. *"Dar a luz*—bring the child forth to the light.''

Caroline couldn't help her sigh of admiration. "What a lovely way to say it."

"It's lovelier when it doesn't mean your ankles

are as swollen as Papi's and you have to pee every five seconds," said Mariela, her voice cheerful.

Elena rose. "I threatened Ramón, told him I was going to clue you in on how this keeps happening." She hugged Mariela, then turned toward Caroline. "Mariela Vargas, this is Dr. Caroline Malone." She hugged the older man. "Papi, you come to let me feed you for a change? Tired of Mami's cooking?"

The older man held Elena close, but Caroline could see fatigue in his face. She glanced down at his feet and saw the swelling above his shoes. She wanted to listen to his heart, run an ECG. She wondered if Diego's equipment extended to an electro-cardiograph.

"Caroline, this is *mi padre*, Trini Vargas," Elena said.

The older man gave her a solemn nod. "So you are *la doctora* who is staying with Diego."

"In his cabin," Caroline clarified. "Just for a month." She waited for him to ask for her help, but he merely smiled.

"Welcome to La Paloma—" He broke off, his face lighting with a broad smile. "Ah, there he is. *¿Qué tal, Diego?*"

Caroline felt him even before she turned around. Needing more equal footing, she rose from her chair as Diego moved up beside her.

He was so tall, so… *Qué padre,* Elena had said,

and she was right. Diego was all man. But he was more.

"Señor Vargas." Diego nodded. "You have brought Mariela for her checkup, I see."

Caroline caught the worried look darting between Mariela and Elena. Elena's stare at Diego, Diego's brief nod.

"Perhaps you will let Dr. Malone listen to your heart while you are here," Diego continued. "She is a heart doctor. Her experience is far superior to mine."

He had no right— Caroline saw hope flare in the eyes of both women and barely clamped down in time on the protest rising to her lips. Diego looked down at her then, but his eyes begged no pardon. Instead, his expression dared her to refuse.

She glanced again at the woman who already felt like a friend, seeing the plea in her gaze. She shot Diego a glare that said they would hash this out later, but then she turned to the older man, holding up her hand. Only fair to warn him. "I'm not able to perform surgery just now, but I would be happy to do what I can."

"*¿Con su permiso?*" Diego left the decision in the older man's hand.

Pride warred with concern in the older man's gaze. Finally, he acquiesced. "After you have seen to our Mariela."

Diego's nod was solemn. "Of course." He turned

to Caroline. "Dr. Malone? Will you accompany us while Elena visits with her father?" Those seer's eyes had never been less repentant.

Caroline's own narrowed. "Of course."

Diego's gesture was all chivalry. "After you, ladies."

Caroline refused to look at him as she followed Mariela. Despite her inner turmoil, however, excitement stirred.

DIEGO SAW his small examining room through Caroline's eyes and wondered what he'd been thinking. She didn't sneer, but her disappointment spoke volumes.

She couldn't know how hard it had been to assemble this poor assortment. The examining table and autoclave had come from a retiring doctor in El Paso. He and Ramón had bartered for the sink and done the plumbing; he'd built the cabinets himself.

He'd been able to talk the hospital in El Paso into taking a tax write-off for donating their outdated X-ray machine, and it would be arriving soon. He'd have to develop film the old way, but it was an important step. He spent nights working on the new clinic, hoping to have space ready as soon as it arrived.

But he looked at everything anew through the eyes of Caroline Malone, and he saw the unfinished walls, the worn upholstery on the examining table.

Saw the uneven concrete floor and knew the stir of shame.

And close upon its heels, the anger. She had no right to judge.

Forcibly, he blocked out her presence, wishing he'd never asked her inside but knowing that Ramón's father needed more help than he could provide. He drew in a deep breath and concentrated on the only important person in the room.

Mariela. His patient.

"How are you feeling, Mariela?" He held her hand, in this manner a good student of his grandmother's, understanding that the talking was as important as the examination.

"Fine," she said, darting a glance at Caroline.

"I should have asked you if it was all right for Dr. Malone to be in here."

Caroline leaped at the offer like a lifeline. "I'll just wait outside—"

"No, don't go," Mariela said. "Diego and *la señora* work too hard. It's good of you to help." She smiled. "I don't mind. Really."

Diego saw the deer-in-the-headlights glance Caroline shot in his direction. To her credit, she masked it and spoke to Mariela, holding up her hand. "With this, I can't be much help."

Diego realized that he was not alone in being troubled by shame. "Your knowledge is the only tool we need," he said. "My hands can't replace what's inside your head."

"*Tesoro*," Mariela murmured.

Caroline looked startled. "What does it mean? Elena used that word."

"Treasure," Diego supplied. "Your knowledge and experience are treasures."

Faint color blossomed in her cheeks. She stared at her hand as though seeing it for the first time. Then she glanced up at him, the green eyes not accusing him anymore but soft, instead. "Thank you." She dropped her gaze. "I haven't felt very valuable to anyone lately."

Diego was moved by the vulnerability tracing the lines of her frame. "Your value to us is beyond price," he said softly.

Mariela turned to him, assessing.

Diego cleared his throat. "So now tell me truthfully, Mariela. Just how tired are you of waiting?"

Mariela chuckled. "Today would be good. Yesterday would have been better."

Diego grinned. "Are you resting when the little ones nap?"

"I try," she said. "But Ramón, Jr. thinks he's too old for a nap now."

"At the ripe old age of four," Diego sighed. "I know it's not easy with three children, but tell that big lug you're married to that he has to help out."

"He does, really. Ramón works so hard, but at

night he bathes the children and puts them to bed while insisting that I prop up my feet. He does all he can, Diego—you know that.'' She placed her hand on his. ''Mami tries to help, too, but she's so worried about Papi.''

As was Diego. He nodded toward Caroline. ''We have help now.'' He squeezed her hand. ''You just worry about this little one. Lie back and let me check you.''

As he examined Mariela, he talked his way through it with Caroline. Her questions proved that she hadn't forgotten as much as she'd thought.

''Will you come?'' Mariela asked her. ''When it's time, will you come with Diego?''

Caroline's eyes went wide. ''I don't—''

''Not because Diego can't do it. He's great—he delivered our last baby. But he only has two hands, and as good a father as Ramón is, he gets a little—'' Her glance at Diego was filled with laughter as they both recalled Ramón's getting woozy at the sight of blood. ''Mama Lalita wouldn't have to come if you were there.''

Caroline stared at her damaged hand. ''I can't—'' She darted a look at him, then back at Mariela. ''I might already be gone.''

''You'd better not be. If I have to be pregnant for another month, no one around here is safe.'' Mariela's dark eyes danced.

The uncertainty painting Caroline's face stirred

protective instincts in Diego, but he knew only too well that striving to break past limits was the only way to gain confidence in your impaired abilities. He hadn't realized how deeply her faith in herself had been shaken. She needed to learn that whether or not she could do surgery again, she had value.

So he remained silent and let Caroline deal with her fears.

Mariela was not only a good mother but a wise woman. "Whatever will be, will be. If you're here, though, we would welcome you. We'd be grateful for any assistance you could provide Diego." Phrased that way, there was pressure, yes, but there was also acceptance of limits.

Caroline still looked worried, but she found a small smile. "I'll try."

"Thank you," Mariela said. Then she turned her attention back to Diego. "Now, I'm begging you, tell me that I'm dilating and this is almost over."

Diego stood and removed his gloves. "Will it help if I tell you there is some thinning of the cervix and the head is down?"

Mariela closed her eyes and moved her lips. Then she opened her arms and grasped him in a fierce hug. *"¡Gracias a Dios!"* She kissed him smack on the lips. "If I weren't married, I'd fall in love with you. Help me off this table. I'm going to go kiss my husband."

Diego helped her down. "You might want to

watch out for that kissing. It seems to lead to other things.''

Mariela's hair swung around her shoulders as she winked. ''I know.'' Moving surprisingly fast for a woman so pregnant, she disappeared.

He and Caroline traded smiles.

Then hers faded. ''Diego, I—''

He held up a hand. ''It was wrong of me to force your hand, but I need your help. Please take a look at Trini. I'm worried about him, but he refuses to go to the doctor. He's scared they'll put him in a hospital, and in his mind, people only go to hospitals to die.'' He held her gaze. ''I'm past my limits on this one. I suspect chronic heart failure, but I just can't be sure with no more equipment than this.'' He glanced around the room, trying not to see it again through her eyes.

''I'm not a cardiologist, Diego.''

''I know chronic heart failure can't be cured surgically, but you've had the same cardiology training.''

She studied him, then seemed to come to a decision. ''No ECG nearby?''

He shook his head. ''I have a shot at buying one, but it will still be two months until the hospital in Fort Stockton replaces theirs.''

''You can't be sure it's CHF without one. Even I can't do that. What about an X ray?''

''I talked a hospital in El Paso into donating one,

but it will be two weeks—if I get the place finished to put it.''

''I'm impressed,'' she said. ''How'd you manage the donation?''

He smiled. ''Good old-fashioned guilt.''

''They didn't want to send a site team? Investigate your credentials? Check out your back molars?''

''Well…'' He shrugged. ''It's the base hospital. A retired general there seems to think he owes me.''

''Ah.'' Mischief sparked in those green eyes. ''Connections.''

He nodded. ''The military is a family. It doesn't forget its own.''

Something faint and sad tripped across her delicate features, and he wondered what it was.

She shook it off the way a dog dispels water. ''Well, we'll just have to make do with what we have. Let's take a look at Mr. Vargas.''

Inside him, a burden eased. He loved Trini Vargas like a father. He'd tried everything he knew to get him to more specialized medical care, and the failure to accomplish it weighed on him every day. Maybe she would have a better answer than his own diagnosis.

''Thank you,'' he said, looking down at her. Wishing he dared to touch her.

Her eyes went dark; her voice, crisp. ''Don't

thank me yet. They used to call me Miracle Malone, but I've been out of miracles for a long time now.''

''I don't expect one.''

''Yes, you do,'' she said. ''Just remember, I warned you.'' She walked to the sink to wash her hands.

Before he went to fetch Trini, he turned. ''Do they know you're not so tough as you pretend?''

''I do my share of pro bono work,'' she admitted, her stance turning to challenge. ''But don't ever assume I'm pretending. I'm as tough as I have to be.''

He wondered how many times in her life she'd had anyone on whom to lean. He kept his voice soft. ''You don't have to be tough here, Caroline. We won't hurt you.''

Leaving her staring at him, he left the room.

AFTER TRINI VARGAS DEPARTED, Diego shook his head. ''I'd hoped I was wrong.''

''I can't be sure,'' Caroline said. ''I need more tests. We've got to get him to a hospital. I want ECG and an echo test—''

''He won't go, I told you.'' The pale eyes had turned grim. ''Mama Lalita makes him a dandelion tea. It seems to have helped with the swelling.''

''What is that—some form of diuretic?''

''Yeah. And she's convinced him to alter his diet. But it's not enough.''

''He may need beta blockers. I want to run an

angiogram—damn it.'' She saw the same frustration in his eyes and pushed harder. ''Diego, this is barbaric. We can't just let him—''

''Die?'' One dark eyebrow rose. ''He's going to die anyway. All of us are.''

''How can you just—'' She whirled away, then back, glaring. ''Why did you ask me if you weren't going to do something about it?''

''Life has seasons, Caroline. It's always changing its rhythms. Only man tries to bend life to his will, but in the end he's doomed.''

''Do you really believe that?'' She stared at him. ''Why did you fight so hard to come back, then?'' Watching his eyes narrow, she pushed again. ''Maybe Adelaida has reached that level of serenity, but you haven't, have you?'' When his eyes widened, she knew she'd hit a nerve. ''That's why you're still here. Why you want to build a clinic. You're a warrior, Diego, no matter where you are.''

''No,'' he snapped. ''I'm not. I can't be—''

''The best healers are fighters,'' she said, the truth of it sinking in. ''We take on death hand to hand. With our teeth and nails, if need be.'' Power surged through her as it had so many times when she'd held a human heart in her palm and brought it back to life.

The sweet memory of triumph lifted her head, straightened her spine. She looked up at Diego with a certainty she hadn't felt in a long, long time. She gripped his hand. "You know that feeling, don't you? You've beaten back death, too."

Memory sparked hot in his eyes. Power flared between them. She felt his strength and her own.

Just as quickly, sorrow smothered the sparks. Despair settled over his shoulders like a shroud. He pulled his hand from hers, and his strength with it. "I don't fight anymore, Caroline." He turned away, moving toward the door. "I'll give you a ride back to the cabin."

She stared after him, her first instinct to let him go. That something troubled him so should be no concern of hers. Prying wasn't like her. She wasn't the sympathetic-shoulder type.

But it bothered her, this sense of some great sorrow inside him. It was more than just losing his career, she thought. More than physical scars.

He hadn't made his peace with this life, no matter how everyone obviously needed and wanted him here. The destiny Adelaida was so sure of hadn't settled inside him; it still clung to a precarious balance on his shoulders, more weight than blessing.

"Show me where you want to put your clinic?" The question surprised Caroline almost as much as Diego.

In the process of picking up her purchases, he stopped. "What?"

"Elena told me about your clinic. I want to see it."

"Why?"

Why did she, except to try to understand a man who would soon be only a memory? "Never mind."

He studied her. "I can't do it today. I have to run some errands after I drop you off." He headed out the front door to his pickup.

"Patients," she surmised.

He shrugged. "Just…friends who need help."

"Are you licensed at all?"

"No."

The risks were breathtaking, but surely he knew that. "What would that require?"

He hesitated, eyebrows drawn together. "I have training equivalent to a P.A."

"Physician's assistant? Really? Where did you get your training?"

"Eighteen months at a special joint operations medical center at Fort Bragg. I'm qualified to handle a whole laundry list—gunshot wounds, burns, field surgery, anesthesia, delivering babies—you name it."

She thought about it a minute. "So…most everything a physician can do."

He nodded. "Everything but write prescriptions."

"But you need a supervising physician, right? Do you have one?"

"No."

"Have you tried?"

Stacking her purchases on the seat between them, he glanced over at her. "Are you offering?"

"Me?" She drew back. "I couldn't—"

"I know, I know," he said. "You won't be here. You're going to get your life back."

Her heart beat a little too fast. "You don't believe I will? You did it. Adelaida told me they said you'd never walk again, but you proved them wrong."

His patient gaze held too much of pity. He started the engine and pulled away. "I'm not jumping out of airplanes on rescue missions, Caroline." He paused as if to say something more, then shook his head and looked straight ahead.

"What?" she asked.

"Nothing."

Something in her wouldn't let the topic go, even though the last thing she wanted to do was discuss his obvious belief that her career was finished. "You don't think I can do it, do you?"

She saw a muscle in his jaw jump. "I would never say that to you." When he turned, those eerie eyes blazed. "Even knowing very little about you, I know you've fought long odds before to make it to where you are. I know you've got guts and brains and heart—"

Fury rocketed around the cab, making the air hot and hard to breathe, but mingled with it was something she would think about later. Something that felt a lot like pride. She hadn't known pride in a very long time, and she drank it in like precious water in the desert.

"Is there a 'but' in there somewhere?" she asked, holding her breath, realizing that Diego's opinion mattered much more than it should.

He let out his own breath in a gust. Stopping the pickup in front of her cabin, he turned to face her. "Not a *but*, not exactly."

She opened her mouth to protest, but he held up a hand. "I think if anyone can make it back, it's you. I don't know what all those battles were that you fought before, but you didn't have anything handed to you, did you?"

"No." She'd never had anyone who really understood. The relief that he might be one who did was almost dizzying. "No, I didn't."

His eyes were so gentle when they looked at her. "Your will has been enough to get you past all those barriers, but you've been a doctor long enough to know that sometimes all the will in the world isn't enough."

She pulled her gaze away from his, blinking. "It will be. I just—I got in too big a hurry—I see that now," she said in a rush, as if she could outrun his logic. "I'll be more patient when I go back, and I won't fight them on any of it—"

His hand on hers halted her in her tracks. Its warmth and comfort made her want to curl up in his lap and weep. "Caroline," he said. "If you won't let me help, talk to Mama Lalita. Your brain and your heart are fighting, and your hand is the battleground.''

He didn't say she wouldn't make it. She clung to that. "Herbs won't fix my hand."

He sighed, but he didn't let go. She didn't want him to. "Your surgeon's mind won't help now. Let go of it, just while you're here."

"But a surgeon is who I am—" *It's all I am*, she thought. That had always been enough, and she didn't like feeling that was wrong.

"You've let it be who you are. You've told yourself it's all you need because it was all you'd let yourself have." Those mage's eyes saw too deeply into her. "What about love, Caroline?" His voice walked right down inside her and made her feel too much. "What about family? You don't want to be alone forever, do you?"

She pulled her hand away and faced the front. "It's not smart to depend on anyone but yourself. In the end, we're all alone. We just kid ourselves that things are different."

"We *are* alone." That he didn't argue surprised her. "But facing that doesn't mean that we have to give up what makes life good—family and friends and love. There's no reason to deny yourself. There's room for all of it."

She wrapped her arms around herself. "But everything can be taken away," she whispered. "Love can disappear."

"Who was taken away from you, *mi bonita?*"

Everyone. She blinked several times, locking her jaw against speaking of her family. She would break down, and she needed all her strength now. "It doesn't matter. You have to get on to your patients." She reached for the door handle, but his hand gripped her chin and turned her to him.

"If you can't trust me, please trust my grandmother," he said, his eyes as soft and dark as velvet, as sorrowful as the waning of a long, gray day.

She wanted to. More than she'd ever imagined. "I—" She tried to tell him all the reasons she couldn't, but she was feeling too much and it hurt more than she could stand.

He released her chin but laid that hand against her cheek. She could feel the calluses and the strength in his fingers. She wanted to seek shelter in his embrace and find the respite that had eluded her for so long.

"Sh-h," he soothed. "Let it go. Allow your heart to rest, just for a little while." He leaned forward and placed his forehead against hers. Under his breath, he murmured in Spanish, and it sounded like prayer.

Peace slid into her, a peace different from the one she felt at Adelaida's but no less comforting. The solace of immense power, the knowledge of shared sorrow. He understood her in a way no one ever had, and his compassion poured into the empty places inside her until she wanted to cry out, to latch on. To hold fast—

Fear hit her then, and she recoiled from its slap. The slide into intimacy was too quick. He wouldn't be there for her; he couldn't be. He belonged here and she didn't. She would go back and he would stay. He had many people who depended on him and he would never desert them.

She averted her gaze from his, knowing that she would see sorrow. Hoping pity didn't taint it.

As she fumbled with the door handle, she grappled for the composure that had once been second nature, dragging her worn, tarnished shields back in place around her to protect the heart he touched too easily.

She wouldn't run away, no matter how she wanted to do so. Drawing upon every ounce of control she could manage, she stepped from the pickup. ''Thank you for the ride,'' she said with a voice that sounded false even to her ears.

After a very long pause, he nodded. ''You're welcome.''

She clasped the quilt to her chest and watched him drive away.

Wishing it weren't so foolish to want to ask him to stay.

CHAPTER SEVEN

"SAM, I NEED some of your magic."

"Caroline—" Her hospital administrator's surprise turned to caution. "How are you doing?"

"How do you think I am stuck in Outer Mongolia?"

"You need the rest," he said. "You were pushing too hard."

"If I get any more rest I might as well become a vegetable."

"Are you truly miserable or is this just carping?"

She paused, then sighed. "Some of both, I guess. I don't belong here. I'm going nuts with no car."

"You were going nuts around here, too," he reminded her. "How's the hand?"

She looked down. "I can't tell." And it sank in her gut like a stone. "Damn it, Sam, what about my patients? No one will talk to me."

"Caroline, we agreed—" Frustration slid into regret. "Everyone's being taken care of."

It was what she hoped—and feared. "Judd's got

to be delirious. He's the man now. Got me out of his way—'' To her horror, her voice wobbled.

Sam sighed. ''He's a very competent surgeon, you know that. He'll do his best for your patients, and—'' A pause. A long one. ''We've got a new guy arriving soon.''

''New guy—'' Caroline's ears rang with her terror. ''You've replaced me? Sam, I'm going to get better. You have to believe that. I'm—oh, man, I'm coming back now. Right now, do you hear me?'' She hated how her voice had turned shrill. With effort, she lowered it. ''You can't do this. I've got a contract. You need me.''

''Listen to me, and stop freaking out.'' In his voice she heard the administrator now, not the friend. ''We need help. We're not looking to replace you. This guy wanted a one-year position for personal reasons—''

''A year?'' she exclaimed. ''It's not going to take me a year—''

He broke in. ''No one's saying you will, but you can't be sure how long you'll be out of commission and neither can we. Your caseload was always heavy. Judd can't handle all your patients and his, too—you know that.'' Another pause, then the friend spoke again. ''Swear to God, no one's looking to replace you. We couldn't if we wanted to—there's only one Miracle Malone.''

She wrapped her free arm around her waist and

bent double, trying to still the trembling. "Oh, God, Sam, why did this happen?" she whispered. "Was it pride? Did I deserve this?"

"No one deserves it," he said, sounding tired. "Listen, Caroline, we're all just doing the best we can. No one wants you back in shape more than me. You're missed by everyone around here."

She pictured Judd Carter and rolled her eyes. "Yeah, I just bet."

He chuckled. "All right, so you were no saint, but you go the distance and then some for every patient, and the entire staff respects that." He paused. "Even Judd Carter."

She cleared her throat of the sudden fullness. "I miss it so much, Sam."

"I know you do." They were both silent for a time. "So what's this magic you want from me?"

"I want an ECG machine. Doesn't have to be cutting edge."

"What's this about? What are you doing? Damn it, Caroline, you're supposed to be resting."

Sam Calvert never swore. "It's not for me."

"Who, then?"

How to explain Diego Montalvo? "You know the caretaker you told me about? How come you didn't tell me the cabin belonged to him?"

"I didn't know. What's he got to do with this?"

She thought about trying to tell him about Adelaide, but she didn't trust him not to sneer.

Like you did, Caroline?

"He's a former medic. Special Forces. Lots of advanced training. The people around here have no health-care options closer than a hundred thirty-five miles and no money to get care, anyway. He's trying to build a clinic to help them, but he's having to scrounge up his equipment. The ECG isn't all he needs, but there's one patient—"

"Where's his funding coming from?"

"His pocket, best I can tell."

"Who's supervising him? What's his certification?"

She laughed then. "Sam...none of that applies out here. You have no idea what this place is like. It's almost a Third World country."

"You have a contract with Mercy, Caroline. Any lawsuits would spill over onto us. I can't allow that."

She knew he was right. Hadn't she made similar points about liability to Diego? Still, something in her rebelled. "I told you I'm not involved. There's no jeopardy to the hospital. Diego doesn't even know I'm doing this."

"Why are you?" he asked.

She paused, wishing she herself knew.

"Never mind," he chuckled. "I shouldn't even ask the same woman who's talked me into more pro bono patients than a sane man should allow." He was quiet for a second, and she could hear a pen tapping on a desk. "Okay. We don't have one to spare, but I seem to recall that Northwest was looking to acquire some equipment from us. I'll see what they might be willing to trade."

"How soon? I need it right away, Sam. There's this old man—"

"You said you weren't involved."

"He's Diego's patient, but I want to help somehow. Diego is fighting an uphill battle."

"Diego, huh? And you're living in his cabin?"

"He doesn't live there. Get your mind out of the gutter."

"It's not in the gutter. An affair would be good for you. God knows you deserve some fun after all you've been through."

The affection in his voice almost undid her. They'd gone toe-to-toe when he'd arrived at Mercy, but he'd become her staunchest advocate. "I'm not having an affair."

"Well, think about it. If he's a good guy, that is."

"He's got his own problems, but yeah," she said. "He's a good guy."

"So—" Sam said. "Enough touchy-feely for me. I'll see what I can do on the machine."

Caroline laughed at his discomfort. "Thanks, Sam." Then a smile curved her lips. "And while you're looking, here are a few other things Diego could use."

Sam groaned, but he made a list.

SHE AWOKE from her nap in stages, caught in a dream of a time before her father left them, a rare day when she'd had his notice and felt the warm sun of his approval. She'd been in the seventh grade honors program and had taken the Preliminary SAT. She'd been recognized by Duke University as exceptional.

They were having a special dinner in her honor. Her favorite foods of the time: *fajitas* and her mother's scrumptious cherry pie. With Ivy's help, Chloe had made her a crown.

All was right with the world: her mother was smiling; her sisters, excited. Her father's regard focused on her, so heady she felt she could float to the ceiling like the balloon that had escaped from the bunch he'd brought home and tied to her chair.

A dog barked. The dream vanished.

Caroline rolled to her side, curling to hold on to it.

Her book hit the floor. Her eyes flew open.

Outside, she heard a voice, low and soothing. Dulcita's excited yap. The shuffle of a horse's hooves, the jingle of a bridle.

She stretched and yawned. What was it about this place that kept her forever napping?

She rose from the sofa, padded to the kitchen window and looked outside.

And sighed.

Diego's Appaloosa stamped the ground, seeking

to divert the man's attention from the foal Diego was speaking to in a low, soothing voice.

Lobo sat nearby, ears at attention, regal as he ignored Dulcita nudging at his side.

All of them vying for Diego's notice, just as she and her sisters had vied for her father's.

But Diego was different. Instead of withholding himself, he made time for each of them, roughhousing Lobo, chivalrous with the elderly Dulcita. Hands gentle on the skittish colt, strong and affectionate with his own mount.

His hands…always his hands drew her. Comforting but firm. Caring and sure. Seductive.

She couldn't take her eyes off him.

Behind the many guises, what did he want for himself? Since he'd lost the life he'd planned, what were his dreams now?

Diego glanced up as if he'd heard her, eyes piercing the half-opened window between them.

Caroline lifted her hand in greeting.

Diego smiled, and her heart stumbled.

Yes, he was dangerous; she sensed that deep in her soul. Too much about him was a mystery, too much unsettled.

But in a way unlike any man before him, Diego Montalvo called to her. Made her aware of herself as a woman.

An affair would be good for you. She should run

screaming. Should slam the door and turn the locks. An affair was something she didn't have time for—

Who was she kidding? She had nothing but time.

But—

Instinct stirred. This man was too complex, too compelling. He wouldn't be ignored, the way she'd always ignored men before when her career beckoned. If she was bold enough to take the lure he cast, she couldn't be sure he'd be easily set aside when convenient.

A faint smile curved her lips.

No, there was nothing easy about Diego Montalvo. He exuded power as surely as he breathed. He had his own battles he did not admit, his own wounds not yet healed, but she'd better not take him lightly.

Healer and warrior, troubled by a destiny he had not yet embraced but too principled to turn away from the needs of others, no matter how they burdened him.

If she had a brain in her skull, she'd lock the doors, draw the drapes and stay very, very far away.

But he fascinated her, and Caroline had always liked a puzzle.

She drew herself a glass of water and drank deeply, giving herself time for reason to win.

Then, more like the woman she'd always been, she set the glass down and walked to the door.

WHEN SHE DISAPPEARED from the kitchen window without acknowledging him, Diego understood that he should be glad.

He *was* glad, damn it. She was brittle and thin and a basket case. She complicated too much, just when he'd begun to find peace.

He stroked the foal from head to tail again and again, letting the little guy play and shiver, his dam watching from a few feet away, cropping grass as if Diego didn't have his hands all over her baby.

"He's a pistol, isn't he, *mamacita?*" Diego walked around to the colt's other side, keeping one hand on the rump as he moved behind the colt to let him know his location when he was out of sight.

The colt kicked once, and Diego spoke to him in Spanish, keeping his tone calm and easy, his hands soothing. "Oh, yes, Mama. He's going to be a challenge, this one."

"You like challenges, don't you?"

Caroline's voice and Lobo's bark sent the colt dancing against Diego's bad hip. He grunted with the pain and shifted but never stopped stroking.

When he had the colt settled again, he met her gaze.

"I'm sorry," she said, glancing at Lobo, whom she'd given wide berth. "I thought I spoke softly enough not to spook him."

Diego shrugged. "It's all right. This one's more high-strung than most."

She didn't answer, and he looked up. Lobo stood at attention. She didn't take her eyes off the dog.

"Lobo," Diego reminded him, "friend."

Lobo peered at him, then at her, still not sure. Dulcita waddled over and plopped down beside Caroline, closing her eyes in bliss as Caroline scratched behind her ears.

"Well, one of them trusts me, anyway." She smiled, her gaze returning to the colt and lingering.

"Come on in," Diego said. "I can tell you want to pet him."

"Is it that obvious?"

He smiled back. "When you love horses, there's no substitute." He nodded at Dulcita, acknowledging her slavish attention. "Even the most shameless dog can't compete."

Caroline laughed, free and easy as he'd never heard her. He wanted to freeze time and rewind.

"Do it again."

"What?" She looked startled. "What did you say?"

He hadn't realized he'd urged it out loud. "Nothing." The colt danced beneath his hands, feeling Diego's unrest. "Sh-h, little one, it's all right," he soothed. *"Soy loco."* I'm crazy.

Was he ever.

Caroline hadn't moved.

He looked up and realized that Lobo had once

again put himself between Diego and her. "Lobo—" he snapped. "Down."

As though he sensed how much Caroline disturbed Diego, Lobo obeyed with obvious reluctance. Caroline glanced back at Diego, then again at Lobo, as if she couldn't decide who posed the greater danger.

His own unease had him bristling. "Never mind. Go back inside if that's what you want."

"That's not—" Caroline cursed with an aptitude that would have made any soldier proud.

Taken by surprise, Diego laughed.

"What's so funny?" She stared at him.

"You." He shook his head, still chuckling. "I can't figure you out."

"Me?" At first she appeared to be offended, but soon enough a smile slid over her features as she shook her head. "I'm not the mysterious one."

Why that felt like a compliment he couldn't pinpoint. He shrugged. "No mystery here. I'm just a simple man."

Laughter burst from her lips. Diego stopped, his hand on the colt, and stared at her this time, frank in his appreciation.

Her smile lingered. "You are the least simple man I ever met." The look in her eyes made him wish, for one insane moment, that he could forget all the reasons she was off-limits.

"Well..." He cleared his throat, tearing his gaze

from hers as though he were a green kid. He barely
resisted the urge to shuffle his feet.

Madre de Dios.

Before he could figure out what to say to her, she
spoke. "I do want to pet that colt." She glanced
over at Lobo, then back at him.

Diego started to rescue her, but she surprised him.

She pulled in a deep breath and took a step—but
not toward him. Toward Lobo.

Diego held his breath as he watched. Lobo's eyes
were wary, his whole body tense. Diego wished he
could place himself between them, because he
wasn't absolutely sure the dog wouldn't take a piece
of her—

But one look at the resolve in her gaze kept him
silent, praying. *Give her a chance, boy. She won't
hurt you.*

Caroline lowered herself to her knees as she
neared the dog, injured hand tucked against her
body, extending her left hand with excruciating
slowness. "Friend, Lobo," she said in barely a mur-
mur. "I won't hurt you—I promise."

Lobo never took his yellow wolf's eyes from her.
His whole body trembled. Even Dulcita didn't in-
terfere.

Diego was on the verge of ordering her off—

Then, in a movement so slow it took a minute to
register, Lobo lowered his head just the slightest
inch—

And accepted the touch of Caroline's hand.

Diego let out the breath he'd been holding. Let his muscles relax, inch by inch. Hoped his heartbeat would soon resemble something near normal.

Then Caroline turned, her face glowing, and his heartbeat sped up again.

"So beautiful," she said with wonder.

"Yeah." But he wasn't thinking about the dog. This Caroline, relaxed and triumphant, packed a punch he wouldn't soon forget. He wondered if this reaction was all over his face.

Good thing Caroline had already turned away, stroking Lobo and crooning as the big dog scooted his body closer to her hand. Dulcita crowded near to get some of the attention, and Caroline laughed, bringing her damaged hand out from its protection so she could pet them both.

Diego watched like a proud father, his throat thick and his heart full of wonder.

Caroline rose, giving one last pat to each, then headed in his direction, her steps surer than he'd ever seen them, her eyes bright with joy.

Diego knew in that instant that he'd never faced a danger quite like her.

He'd lived like a monk for a long time now, his heart too weighted down with the loss of his men and the fight to make a new life. He'd known he'd get around to women again at some point. His appetites had always been strong.

But he'd imagined that when that day came, he'd have an affair with no strings, some woman with similar appetites who'd be his reintroduction to the land of men and women. And maybe someday, if he was very lucky, he'd find a simple woman who would understand the call of this place and honor his limits, who'd accept affection and his promise to be true, who might even give him children and be part of a peaceful, ordinary life.

There was nothing simple about Caroline Malone. He ought to have his head examined for considering—for even one second—playing with fire like this.

But apparently, the man who had lived on adrenaline, who had loved taking risks, hadn't died with his men.

"Are you okay?" Her voice came from right behind him.

He jolted, and the colt shied.

Diego shoved away crazy wonderings and concentrated on calming the colt. "Yeah."

"Oh, aren't you a love?" she crooned, her left hand stroking the colt's head, her right one lingering in midair as though longing to touch, too. When the colt accepted her touch, she moved closer, resting the damaged hand against his withers as she petted and murmured.

His mount snorted, and Diego moved himself a safe space away from her, rubbing Chieftain's nose and leaning against the fence post, watching the two of them. Lobo stuck his head through the fence and licked his hand. Diego accepted the comfort.

Damn. If only she'd stayed prickly.

As if the silence finally registered, Caroline turned. Four sets of eyes observed.

She glanced at each of them in turn.

Except Diego.

She dropped her hands from the colt. "I—I should get back to my reading." She took two steps away, but the colt followed, and butted her back with his head.

Delight replaced caution, and Caroline swung around to pet the colt again.

"You want to go riding?" The second the words were out of his mouth, Diego cursed himself. How much she obviously missed horses shouldn't matter.

But it did.

Hope leaped into her eyes. Then she saw his face and shook her head. "I can't."

"You could ride with me." In for a penny, in for a pound.

"Do you really want to do that?"

He should say no. If only he couldn't see someone younger and more innocent peering out from her eyes. "You said you missed riding."

"You didn't answer my question." Her chin tilted. "I don't want to be a charity case."

"You're not." He turned away. If only it were

that simple. He walked to the gate and opened it, but didn't look back, waiting for her to decide.

Gazing into the distance, he wondered exactly when the hell he'd lost his mind. Physical proximity was not what he needed just now, and sharing a saddle was about as intimate as two people got still wearing clothes.

Busy trying to figure out how to bow out with grace, he jumped when her hand touched his arm. His gaze jerked to hers.

Green eyes held equal parts anticipation and unease. "Thank you. I'd love to ride." She walked past him through the gate, casting one last look back at the colt, who was only a step behind her. She touched his head. "Bye, sweetheart." She looked at Diego. "Does he have a name yet?"

Diego shook his head. "Want to pick one?"

She studied the colt from the other side of the fence, a small smile playing over her lips. "It shouldn't be a babyish name. He's going to be a big bruiser one day, and he needs a name with enough dignity for a champion."

"You really do love horses, don't you?"

"The only thing I love more is practicing medicine."

For a moment, they were both silent. Then Diego spoke. "Yeah." He'd once had his own dreams of med school after the service. "Come on," he said.

"Mounting with one hand would be tough. I'll give you a boost."

She stopped him with another touch. "Diego, I really mean it. Thank you."

"*De nada,*" he replied. But it felt like much more than nothing.

CAROLINE SAT in front of Diego, only too aware of his size and the hard contours of his body, of how he worked to keep some distance between them.

She'd like some of that distance herself, would like to grab the reins and ride this magnificent animal alone, racing flat out across the land.

But riding double, for all its complications, was worlds better than not riding at all. Drawing in a deep breath of mountain air, she looked around. "It's beautiful here. Not in any way I would have expected, but there's this sense of space and possibilities—" She shook her head. "I don't have the right words."

Behind her, Diego's voice rumbled. "You're doing all right."

His breath across her nape made her shiver.

"Cold? Gets cool as the sun drops behind the mountains."

How could she possibly be cold when he was so warm against her?

She sat up straighter. "I'm fine. Maybe we should

go back. It's got to be hard on Chieftain, carrying double.''

''You don't weigh enough to hurt.''

Her mouth quirked. ''One use for being skinny, I guess. My mother used to despair of me ever filling out.''

''Where is she now?''

The grin vanished. ''She died a long time ago.''

''I'm sorry.''

''It doesn't matter.''

''Of course it does. Losing family hurts.''

Something in his voice made her turn. Her shoulder brushed his chest, her lower body pressing against his. She jerked away as if she'd touched a hot stove, but she couldn't create enough room between them.

Silence fell, thick and edgy. Caroline scrambled to unearth the sophisticated, take-charge woman who considered sex merely recreation or the doctor who understood involuntary physical reactions. She could only find a self-conscious schoolgirl she'd never been.

She grasped for any distraction. ''Where's your pottery studio?''

The saddle creaked as he tried to scoot backward. ''Nothing so fancy as a studio. Just a storeroom on the back of my house.''

''Oh.'' *Gee, such wit, Caroline.*

His weight shifted again. Cool air slid behind her

as Diego dismounted. "My house is just around the next bend. Think I'll walk the rest of the way." He glanced back at her from beneath his hat brim. "If I take the reins and lead him, can you hold on to the saddle horn with one hand?"

"Of course." Embarrassment made her stiff.

"Good." He'd already turned away.

"Stop," she said. "Let me get down. I'll walk back." She could slide off a horse without hands.

She didn't count on the uneven ground and stumbled.

In an instant, he was there, steadying her. "You all right?"

His hands were so big and warm and sure; his chest right in front of her, broad and deep. But what sent her spinning was the compassion in his voice.

"Th-thanks—" she stammered. "I'll find my way back." Again she stumbled, and damned the slick soles of her shoes.

"No—" He grasped her by the waist and pulled her close. "Caroline, don't—"

"Let me go," she whispered. "I don't need you. I don't need anyone—"

"You know that's not true," he said, his voice unbearably gentle. "Maybe it's not me you need, but you can't go on this way. You'll break if you don't bend."

He kept his hold on her loose but firm. Supporting more than restraining. Her eyes burned against the longing to let go, just once, to give in to what she'd feared all her life—

"I—can't—" she choked out. "I don't—"

"Sh-h..." Diego drew her into his body, one hand stroking her back, the other cradling her head against his chest. "Cry, *mi linda*. Cry for all that you've lost."

Even as slow tears leaked, she shook her head and tried to summon the strength to pull away. "Crying doesn't fix anything. I'm not weak. I won't be."

He soothed her as he'd gentled the colt, speaking in deep, even tones. "Of course you're not weak, Caroline, but you're running on nerves. You can't get stronger when you're exhausted."

"I've rested too much here."

"You fight peace the way a child fights sleep." He tipped her head and studied her. "What do you think will happen if you let go?"

She stared up into those mage's eyes. "I lose."

"Lose what?"

He saw too much. She tucked her head back against his chest so he wouldn't see more. "Everything," she whispered.

A slight tensing told her he wanted to ask.

To his credit, he didn't. Instead, he stepped away but clasped her hand. "Come with me."

"Where?"

"To my spring." He'd already begun to walk, holding the reins in his other hand.

She could see the price of this day in his gait. "Why don't we sit down."

He turned, saw her glance at his hip. "I know my limits."

"Your limp is worse."

"Some days that happens." He kept walking. To avoid being a drag on him, she hurried to catch up.

"You have a spring of your own? How big—" She fell silent when they entered a clearing and she got her first look at his house.

"Diego…" she sighed. "It's perfect."

He did stop then, smiling down at her. "Thank you."

The log house, two stories high, sat in the clearing as though it had been there forever. On the wrap-around porch, sturdy rocking chairs called out a welcome. She turned and caught her breath at the view he would have. "Oh, mercy."

"Yeah. Sunrise is always an event."

"A cup of coffee…sitting in one of those chairs…" She resisted another sigh. "How can you bring yourself to leave each day?"

He chuckled. "Some days I don't. Come on inside—or wait out here, and I'll bring you a glass of water."

"No, I'll help. I want to see the rest." She followed him up the steps after he tied Chieftain to a porch rail.

But she lingered outside the screen door, looking

at the vista, breathing deeply and filling herself with the glory of it.

Then the door shut, and she turned to follow.

The interior suited him just as well.

Log walls shone gold as honey in the fading afternoon light. A Navajo rug hung on the wall next to a rustic stone fireplace with a thick, rough-hewn wooden mantel. Two butterscotch leather couches flanked the fireplace with another Navajo rug on the floor between them. She spotted a bronze on one table—a warrior on horseback.

The orange of the lowering sun poured through the windows of a kitchen that felt homey. Pine cabinets lent a golden warmth; Lobo's claws clicked on the red Mexican-tile floor. A big window over the sink looked out toward more mountains; beside a round oak table ranged a wall of windows.

A bowl sat on the tile countertop, surely of Diego's design, this time deep cobalt bleeding through an iridescent silver.

Diego turned, holding two glasses filled with icy water, his expression serious and waiting.

She didn't try to hide her wonder. "This place is incredible. How long have you lived here?"

"Off and on for years. Took me six years to build it, working on it when I was on leave."

"You built it?" She turned in a circle. "You did all of this?"

"Every last inch."

She took a sip of the cool, delicious water. "I'm impressed."

He shrugged. "You didn't see all the mistakes I had to redo."

"It's truly stunning, Diego. It feels so..." She searched for the right word.

"Rustic?" he supplied.

"I was thinking that it feels solid and...right. Like a refuge."

His eyes went distant. "It was."

"Was?"

Then she understood. "I'm intruding."

"No." He studied her, his eyes not quite seeing her. He shook his head. "I would have thought so, but...no."

She didn't know what to say to that. She drank again, watching him.

His gaze lingered. When she lowered her glass, he looked at her mouth.

They were three feet apart. Oddly breathless, she wondered who would move first.

Diego turned away and settled his glass in the sink. "You wanted to see where I work," he said, staring out the window.

She shouldn't be this disappointed. "Yes," she replied, striving for cheer.

He gave her wide berth as he led her to the door that opened onto the porch. "This way."

She dispensed with her own glass. "Thank you for the water."

His tone was equally polite. "You're welcome."

He showed her his potter's wheel, described how it worked. Led her to the outdoor kiln and answered her questions.

But the air between them danced with possibilities and desires, with an edgy, yawning hunger.

She didn't know how much longer she could stand it.

When he guided her out the back, she spied the pool of water, licked by tongues of flame from the setting sun. Surrounded by rocks on the back and trees to each side, it was a natural haven no landscape designer could imitate.

Diego's unease told her this was a sacred space and she was trespassing.

"I should go."

He turned slowly. "Why?"

"Because—" She looked up at him. "This is important to you. I'm in the way."

She wished she could decipher what was in those seer's eyes as they locked on hers.

He closed the small distance between them. "You're right. You are in my way—" He shook his head. "But not like you think. You're in my head and I can't get you out." His hand rose slowly and cupped her cheek.

Caroline couldn't find her voice. She closed her

eyes as his fingers traced her cheekbone, her jaw…hovered over her mouth—

Then his lips were a breath away. "You're too complicated, Caroline," he murmured.

"What?" She tried to make sense of his words.

But it was too late. His lips brushed hers, as softly as the petal of a rose. He lifted them and waited—

Her lids flew open. Eyes older than time spoke of danger.

"I don't care." She rose to her toes, sealing her mouth to his, grasping his collar with her left hand to prevent his escape.

Instead Diego growled, and sweet turned hot. Strong arms pulled her against a body tense with suppressed desire.

Reason fled. Her flesh came alive with a scream. It had been so very long since she'd done this—

Diego shifted, drew her closer. Slanted his mouth to go deep.

Correction—she'd never done *this*. Nothing had ever felt so good.

The last of her control slipping, she jerked on his hair, tried to step away. To think. "God—" she gasped, "What's happening?"

Diego's chest heaved as he watched her, still holding her tight. "I don't know—we shouldn't—" He looked as shell-shocked as she felt. His eyes narrowed. "Hell with it." He lowered his head again.

She shot through the tunnel with him, sliding fast

and deep into lunacy, reckless with delight. Warning lights flared at the edge of consciousness, but the lure of him blinded her; the feel of him drove her mad. She rested her injured hand against his chest and let the other hand roam over his broad back. When his hands slid behind her and pressed her close, she knew she wasn't the only one dying for more. She moaned and rubbed against him.

He tore his mouth away. Held her at arm's length, staring at her as if she were some sort of apparition.

"This is wrong," he said.

He was right. It made her furious. "We're both adults. I get tested often. I know I don't carry any diseases and won't get pregnant. If you're safe, then what's the harm?" Though the words fit her past behavior, they left a bad taste in her mouth now.

"I'm safe, but that's not the point. You're not ready, *mi linda,*" he said. "Nor am I."

She cast a glance at the fly of his jeans. "You look ready to me." She didn't know why she was pushing.

"You need a friend, not a lover."

"Love has nothing to do with it. This is only physical."

"Go ahead and think that." His eyes saw too much. They burned past all her defenses.

"Stay away from me," she said, whirling. Misery churned. She was watching someone she'd never met and wondering who the hell she was. "I'll find my way back."

"If that's how you want it." His voice was tight, as raw as her nerves. He held out one hand. "I'll take you home."

"Go to hell, Diego." She slapped it away. "I'm a grown woman. You just go to hell." Then, before she mortified herself any worse, she whirled and ran.

"Caroline," he shouted.

She didn't look back.

DIEGO FOLLOWED HER at a distance on foot, knowing she would hear Chieftain's hooves if he rode, worried she'd run faster and fall as shadows lengthened. He would pay all night for the insult to his hip, but he couldn't let her go alone.

He would pay anyway. Hunger for her gnawed at his insides; loathing swamped his mind. He wanted her, yes, now worse than ever, but he'd known how fragile she was and hadn't been able to stop himself. Just a taste, he'd thought.

Never dreaming how much he'd crave more.

CHAPTER EIGHT

TWO DAYS HAD PASSED with Caroline in hiding, venturing outside only when she was sure she was alone. The hours dragged; she was ready to scream with the boredom. She'd spoken with her lawyer and made arrangements with a private detective to begin looking for Ivy and Chloe. It was time. Her life wasn't back on track, but thoughts of her sisters wouldn't go away anymore.

A chill swept through her. What if she'd waited too long? What if neither wanted to see her? In that moment, longing for Ivy pierced her to the core. Chloe had been very young when she was taken away; they might have nothing in common. But Ivy...surely she hadn't changed so much. *Please, Ivy, still care about your family.*

Caroline leaped up and began to pace. Why should Ivy care when Caroline had had the funds to afford a search for a long time and hadn't done it?

Maybe she should call the investigator back and cancel. She'd had so little information to give him, anyway.

She stared around the cabin that was beginning to feel like a prison. If she was left alone with her thoughts any longer, she'd scream. Last night she'd been reduced to catching talk radio from the border, some wild-eyed evangelist begging for money so he could prevent the end of the world.

She'd never been a coward in her life. She couldn't continue, even if she had no idea what she'd say to Diego the next time she saw him.

Well, the next time she *talked* to him—she'd seen him every day with the colt. Had hung back out of sight like some leper. His limp was worse, and she wondered why he drove himself so.

She wasn't the only one who needed to be busted back to kindergarten. At least this was only her first offense.

She'd performed all her exercises. Spent too many aggravating moments doing the needlework Don had ordered, nearly biting through her lip from frustration. Her efforts looked like a child's—no trace of the beautiful, even stitches that she'd once sutured into her patients' flesh. The latest segment looked better, but she had so far to go.

Then she remembered that Sam had brought in a replacement surgeon, and picked up the needlework to try again.

Her cell phone rang. She lunged for it. "Hello?"

"First ring," Sam said. "Good. You must be resting."

"Going out of my mind is what I'm doing. Talk to me, Sam," she pleaded. "Hospital gossip, patient census, board meeting horrors—I'm desperate. Tell me about supplier problems—I'll be the best audience you ever had."

"That bad, huh?" He chuckled. "Then you must really be behaving."

"Don't tease. Give me a crumb."

Sam took mercy on her and launched into a series of stories—snippets of the life she longed to rejoin. Finally, when he had her laughing over a tale of Judd Carter and the new guy, Wes Hunter, locking horns in the doctors' lounge, he got to the point of his call. "I found you an ECG."

"Ah, Sam, you magician you. Who'd you have to kill?"

"It gets better. Got you a microscope and centrifuge and an obscene number of bandages. Got drug reps to commit for a ton of samples."

"That's it. Divorce Lydia and run away with me to Belize. I think I love you."

Sam chuckled. "I couldn't run fast enough to escape Lydia's wrath."

Caroline thought of the kind woman who was both Sam's comfort and bulwark in a career field filled with far more obstacles than triumphs. Lydia didn't have an ounce of wrath in her. Caroline sighed. "Just my luck. All the good ones are taken."

"I thought you'd agreed to have an affair."

"I said no such thing." She heard her voice go tight at the memory of how she'd all but devoured Diego before she'd recovered her mind.

"What, Helen?" Sam spoke to his secretary, then came back on the line. "Gotta go, kiddo. Recess is over."

She wanted to keep him on the line. Maintain contact with the only world where she knew what she was doing.

But she was sure he'd given her far more time than he could afford. "I'll pay for the shipping. How soon will the stuff arrive?"

"Mercy still has some favors to grant to its best surgeon. The shipping's on us. The stuff should be there the first of next week."

"Sam, I don't know how to thank you."

"Just get well, Caroline, and come back to us. We need you."

The words did much to pour oil on troubled waters. "I'm doing my best. Love to Lydia," she said.

"Hang in there, friend. The month will be over before you know it." Then he was gone.

She disconnected the call and stood there, phone still in hand as though it could keep her old life alive a little longer.

Early next week. Only the second of her four weeks. So long...

She took in a deep breath. But at the end of that

week, she would be halfway through her sentence. She would make it.

Somehow.

It was time to come out of her cave and find Diego. Give him the good news. She set the phone in its charger, reluctant to turn it off just in case someone else from her real life called.

No one had yet, but the hope sustained her.

"All right," she said. "Time to quit licking your wounds and hiding from Diego." She walked into the bathroom and glanced in the mirror.

She looked awful. Her hair was too shaggy, brushing her shoulders in the back. Her skin too pale; her eyes, too lifeless.

Get a grip, Malone. You've been through worse, much worse.

She turned on the shower and began to strip.

A WHILE LATER, she stepped onto the porch of Ramón's store. Diego's pickup was nowhere in sight, but she was too tired to walk back yet. Disgusting how quickly you could get out of shape.

She opened the door. Maybe Elena would know where he was.

She'd only been to this place once, but the smells were familiar now. She'd been welcomed here, been made to feel at home. Her spirits rose.

"Ah, the beautiful *doctora* graces us with her presence." To her left, Ramón greeted her with a big smile. "Come in, come in. Don't be a stranger." He emerged from the aisle where he was stocking cans. "How are you today?"

"I'm...fine." And she realized that, in a way, she really was. She'd done herself no service hiding away, making the cabin a cave. "How are you?"

He leaned over, pitched his voice low. "Mariela is ten months' pregnant, at least in her mind. Take pity on a poor beleaguered husband and don't ask." But his eyes twinkled as he said the words.

Caroline grinned back. "As if you played no part."

He rolled his eyes. "Ah, the things a man forgets when he has a warm and willing woman...I plead insanity. I throw myself on the mercy of the court."

Caroline was laughing when she heard Elena's shout.

"Is he telling you those 'oh, poor me' stories, Caroline? Don't believe a word. He warned Mariela when they married that they would have a dozen children." She walked up beside Caroline. "The idiot woman married him anyway." She threw her arms around Caroline in an easy hug.

Caroline went still. Unused to hugs, she was trying to figure out how to respond long after Elena had released her, chattering on.

"What do you think you're doing, hiding up there like some hermit?" Elena scolded. "Leaving us to deal with Diego?"

"What?" Worry swamped her. "What's wrong with him? His hip is worse, isn't it?"

Elena waved off her questions. "His hip is terrible, of course, but it's never good." Hands fisted at her waist, she continued. "I'm talking about whatever you've done to turn our Diego into a growling bear." She leaned closer, peering into Caroline's face.

Then she smiled. "Ah…I knew it."

Caroline wasn't accustomed to anyone prying into her business. She liked Elena, but this was too much. "Excuse me?" she said in her frostiest voice.

Elena glanced at Ramón. Ramón threw up his hands and backed away. Elena laughed. "Coward," she said to her retreating brother's back.

"I don't know what you're talking about, and furthermore, it's none of your business what happens between Diego and me."

Unperturbed, Elena chuckled again, big silver hoops flashing at her ears, black curls bouncing as her brown eyes gleamed. "I knew it. It had to be something between you two that had Diego's temper on a short leash."

Caroline turned to escape.

Elena grabbed her arm and drew her onto the porch.

"Let go of me," Caroline said, all ice now.

Elena looked again, and amusement fled. "Oh, I'm sorry. I didn't realize."

Despite herself, Caroline had to ask. "Didn't realize what?"

"It's not just Diego, is it? You're hurt, too."

Caroline drew back. "I'm perfectly fine. Now, if
you'll excuse me—"

"I trespassed, didn't I?" She waved her hand.
"Around here, we all live in one another's pockets.
What one knows, everyone knows. We're a family
of sorts, and everyone understands that I speak without thinking sometimes."

Her eyes were sympathetic. "You're not used to
this, I can tell. I—I haven't traveled much." Her
voice vibrated with her longing. "I forget that it's
different in other places. I didn't mean to upset
you."

Thawing a little, Caroline shook her head. "You
didn't upset me."

"Yes, I did, and for that I'm sorry. I like you,
Caroline. I want to be your friend."

When had anyone ever said that to her without
expecting a benefit from it? Touched, Caroline un-
bent but couldn't lie. "I won't be here very long."
She met Elena's gaze. "But...I'd like that, too."
She glanced away. "I haven't had many friends."

Elena grabbed her in another of her spontaneous
hugs, too vibrant to be subdued for long. "Okay,
now that we're friends, I want to know why you're
teasing Diego."

"What?" Caroline had never teased a man in her life.

"Don't get me wrong—it's time someone caught his eye. He's lived like a monk since—" Even Elena couldn't speak lightly of how he'd almost died. "I thoroughly approve. He couldn't go forever without a woman. I give you my blessings to work your charms on him as you will—but the rest of us would appreciate it if you didn't tease him too long."

Caroline couldn't believe what she was hearing. "I'm not—he's not—" What was it with everyone? First Sam tells her to have an affair, then Diego's almost-sister concurs?

Elena burst into laughter. "*Ay, mujer,* if you could see your face right now. Your cheeks are red, your eyes are wide, but…ah, inside those eyes, I see the truth."

Caroline wondered exactly when she'd fallen down Alice's rabbit hole. "What truth?"

"You want our Diego," Elena explained. "He tempts you, and that's very good. He needs to quit crucifying himself over what happened. What better way than to lose his mind over a woman?"

Caroline's mouth fell open. "He won't—he wouldn't lose his mind over me—" She faltered at the very concept, even as it sent a tingle down her spine. Ridiculous. Men didn't lose their minds over her. She didn't even want that.

But a tiny piece of her marveled at the idea.

And reveled in it.

Reason flooded back. "Your imagination is out of control, Elena. First of all, Diego doesn't even like me. Second—" she held out another finger "—I'm not in the market for an affair. I have to focus on getting back in shape to resume my career. Third—"

Elena shook her head. "Are you crazy?"

Caroline jolted. "What?"

"What woman with any brains wouldn't jump at the chance to have that man in her bed?" Then her eyes narrowed. "Is it because of his injuries?" Her voice tightened, her brows lowering. "Or because he's Latino?"

"Don't even say that," Caroline snapped. "You're starting to make me mad." She brandished her hand. "How could I call anyone handicapped when I'm like this?" Her temper rocketed. "And don't you dare call me a bigot. Any man would be proud to have half Diego's intelligence and compassion, to say nothing of what it required to beat the odds of coming back from such severe injuries—"

Elena laughed, holding up a hand. "*Bastante.* Enough. I get the point." Her eyes softened again. "Ah, yes, it would do our Diego good to lose his mind over a woman like you."

Caroline couldn't let Elena keep spinning out this

fantasy. "Elena, Diego is possibly the most intriguing man I've ever met."

Elena nodded.

"But I have no intention of getting involved with him. Even if he were interested, there would be no point."

Elena shook her head, sighing. "Ah, you Anglos. Diego has the same disease. Too much logic and too little listening to the heart." Her eyes glinted with mischief and pity. Her fist smacked against her chest. "Cling to your logic, *mujer,* as you will, but don't be surprised when it does no good. I strongly suspect it's too late for either of you."

Caroline fell silent, not sure how to argue.

Then the irrepressible Elena leaped to the fore. "Ah, well, it's a pretty day, too pretty to be serious." She grasped Caroline's good hand. "Let me feed you lunch, then I'll tell you where to find Diego."

"What makes you think I'm looking for him?"

Elena turned, rolling her eyes. "Please. Let's not ruin a good friendship with unnecessary lies."

Before Caroline could figure out how to counter that, Elena was already pulling her inside with a merry laugh.

DIEGO PAUSED to wipe sweat from his forehead with his sleeve. Working nights as he had up to now, he hadn't had to contend with the heat, but he didn't have that luxury anymore. The X ray would be arriving next week, and he still had Sheetrock to hang and painting to finish.

He lifted the next panel and hammered it into place.

"Diego?"

He whirled at the sound of Caroline's voice.

"Sorry. I didn't mean to startle you," she said, looking as uncomfortable as he felt.

He shrugged. "Couldn't hear you over the hammering."

Silence fell. In it he caught the echo of their last encounter and wanted to ask her what she was doing here, why she'd come out of hiding.

But she looked as though she was about an inch from taking off like a startled doe.

So he waited.

She gestured around the room. "Are you doing this all alone?"

"Sometimes I have help when I'm here at night, but I have to get this finished."

More silence. "Is there anything I could do?"

He cocked his head, trying to figure out what was different about her. She was nervous, yes, but there was some sort of excitement bubbling beneath her discomfort. "Why are you here, Caroline? You told me to stay away."

He'd almost swear it was guilt he saw as she lifted her gaze to his. "I know." She glanced past him.

Shook her head. "I meant it, except that I—" She whirled and began to pace. "Listen to me, will you? I sound like some bumbling teenage girl who doesn't know what she wants. That's not me. I was never a typical teenager. I'm a very competent woman, I'll have you know." She spun to face him, stabbing a forefinger at him. "I can't figure out what to do with you, Diego. You—you bother me."

Laughter fought with frustration. "You're a pain in the ass yourself, Doc."

She stood stock-still, slack-jawed. Then she surprised him by bursting out laughing.

He surprised himself by joining in.

For a moment, Diego felt as good as he had in years, light and free as the boy he'd once been.

Eyes still bright with laughter, she studied him. "We should just jump each other's bones and get it over with."

Damn. He could like her. "That's your professional opinion?"

She grinned. "Nothing professional about how you make me feel." The grin turned wry. "I don't remember a man ever making me want him as you do."

Desire hit him hard then, knocking his control to the ground and shattering it into little pieces. "Come here," he growled, reaching for her.

Caroline danced away, one palm up in warning. "Wait—"

"Waiting's over, Caroline." He dropped his hammer to the floor and stalked her. Forget how he knew it was foolhardy. He was long overdue for a mistake like this.

He grasped her shoulders and brought her against him.

"Diego, I—"

"Did you mean it?" He was already lowering his head to that mouth he'd thought about too much. "You want me?"

She was breathless, her hands roaming over him even as her gaze jittered with need and something else he couldn't identify. "Yes. Oh, yes—" Then she wrapped herself around him as a vine encircles a tree.

She felt so good, he reflected as he kissed her. So right. Insanely perfect.

Then his mind went on vacation. When Caroline moaned and pressed closer, he cursed fate that they were in a building with no locks in the middle of the day in a village where no one treasured privacy the way he did…the way he was sure she did.

He tore himself away, breathing hard. "Not here," he said. "Damn it, not here. Not the first time."

She stared at him, her own chest rising and falling fast. "I—we—" She stepped back, wrapping her arms around herself as she closed her eyes and shook her head as if grappling for good sense.

"Don't do that," he demanded.

"What?" She looked at him, confusion swirling with need and rapidly returning logic.

"We're through dancing, Caroline," he warned. "This is the wrong place for what I have in mind, but we're not finished. You're not running away again, and I'm through being noble. I don't know what the hell this is between us, but I want the time to find out. We'll finish this—don't think we won't."

"Sex," she said, wrapping her arms more tightly. "It's just sex. Just ordinary lust. We need to get it out of our systems and move on."

That should be exactly what he wanted, too. Instead he got madder than hell. "You just keep thinking that." He advanced on her. "But you'd better get a running start back toward Dallas if you intend to hold on to those illusions for long."

He could see the temper sparking. "You can't seriously believe that we—" Then, as though a switch had been flipped, fury gave way to excitement. She grabbed his arm. "I almost forgot why I came over." Her fingers squeezed. "I've got great news for you."

"What?" He couldn't keep up with the lightning-fast shift. "What are you talking about?"

Joy bubbled up, lighting her whole face. "I've got you an ECG and a microscope and a centrifuge and—'' She rattled off a list of supplies, all but vibrating with excitement.

''You what?'' He blinked. ''Whoa. Slow down. Tell me again.''

So she did. At the end of her recital, he could only stare at her. ''How did you do that?''

Caroline's smile widened. ''I called in chips and played on guilt and made Mercy live up to its mission statement of helping those in need.''

''Mercy Hospital?''

''Yeah.'' She grinned. ''And they're throwing in the shipping. The equipment can be here next week.'' She was practically bouncing on her toes.

Diego was trying to take it all in. ''I don't know what to say.'' He looked down at her, wishing he could do something to make her smile like that again. ''You're amazing.'' He looked around him. ''I thought it would take me months, if not years, to gather—''

He grabbed her by the waist and lifted her into a spin, gratitude rendering him speechless. His bad hip faltered; he stumbled but caught her and slid her down his body.

She rendered his embarrassment harmless as she raised her hands to his face. ''It's been so long since I've felt useful,'' she said. ''I've missed it.''

''Caroline,'' he said, holding her gaze with his. ''I don't know what to say. How to thank you.''

''You just did,'' she whispered.

Then they were there again, in that place known only to the two of them. Slowly he lowered his mouth to hers.

"Diego," Elena's worried shout startled them both. "Where are you?"

"Damn." He wondered if he looked as chagrined as Caroline did. "I'm in the back room." Reluctantly, he let Caroline go but caught her hand in his. Lowering his voice, he spoke to her. "Don't go anywhere."

She shook her head, eyes round. "No, I won't."

Elena burst into the room. "It's Mariela," she gasped. "It's time, Diego."

He struggled to shift gears. "Okay. Tell Ramón I'll be right there." He ran through a mental list of what he needed but paused, turning to Caroline. "Come with me," he urged.

Her gaze wavered for a minute, and he held his breath, surprised at how much he wanted her with him.

"Diego, I—" He waited for her refusal.

To his surprise, she nodded. "What do we have to take?"

He pressed a quick kiss to her lips. "Don't forget where we were."

A blush stained her cheeks. "I won't."

WHEN THEY REACHED the small brick house, Ramón greeted them at the doorway, eyebrows lifting as he caught sight of Caroline. "Thank you for coming."

"Have you called my grandmother?" Diego asked.

"Not yet," Ramón answered.

"Mariela is special to her," Diego said. "Call her, but tell her Caroline is with me, and we'll be fine."

Caroline whipped her head around. "Diego, I—"

A slight shake of his head stopped her. "Go ahead, Ramón," he said easily. "Where are the other kids?"

"With my mother." Ramon scrubbed his face. "You'd think I'd be used to this by now, but—"

Diego smiled and clapped his hand on Ramón's shoulder. "You love her, *amigo*. Worry is natural."

"Yeah." Ramón nodded. His mouth turned up in a wry grin. "She wants them, you know—all these babies. It's not just me, despite what Elena says."

"You raise good children," Diego said. "You love them and take care of them. They will make the lives of others better because they've been cherished. The world needs more people like you two."

Ramón still seemed unsettled.

"She'll be fine," Diego insisted. "Go call Mama Lalita, then come hold your wife in your arms. We'll get this baby born."

She saw moisture glisten in Ramón's eyes. "I can't stand this part. I don't like it that something so beautiful requires such pain."

"Beauty comes with a price. Mariela is willing to pay it." Caroline heard the compassion of friend to friend. The comfort of healer to patient. "She knows she is loved. That your children have a protector. Not all children are so lucky, *compadre*."

It was exactly the right thing to say. The tension in Ramón's shoulders eased.

"All right." Ramón drew in a deep breath as if for strength. "Okay. Go to her, Diego. I'll call your grandmother, then I'll be right there."

Such love, Caroline thought. What must that be like, to have a man love you so much that he wants to bring forth life with you, yet is consumed by worry over the cost to you, the woman he loves?

"Ready?" Diego asked, his eyes intent on hers. "If you don't want to do this, now is the time to say so."

Was she? She'd attended births as an intern years ago but had already been certain her path lay elsewhere. Arrogant and sure that delivering babies was for those with lesser skills.

But she thought of Adelaida, of how slowly she moved, of the aches that must plague her joints. Caroline was as rusty as anyone could be, but she was younger and stronger, even with only one good hand.

And anyway, Diego was the expert here. All she

needed to do was be a good gofer. If she was honest, she'd admit to curiosity about how this would be handled outside hospital walls. "Ready as I'll ever be," she answered.

He searched her face, then nodded. "All right. Mariela's an experienced mother, but giving birth is never easy. Just stay calm, and I'll do the rest."

Part of her bristled. Cool under pressure was her middle name. They didn't call her the Ice Queen for nothing. "I'm not a medical student." She couldn't quite keep the insult out of her voice. "Let's get on with it."

His mouth quirked. "Point taken."

Caroline followed him into a small bedroom, where instead of finding Mariela ensconced on the bed she saw her pacing. "About time," she muttered, then grabbed the bedpost for support as pain tightened her face.

Diego's voice remained calm. "I thought perhaps this time you'd just call me and tell me if it was a boy or girl."

After a pause while Mariela gripped the wood and panted, she spoke. "I would," she muttered, jerking her head toward the door. "But that idiot thought we needed help."

Diego chuckled. "Watching the woman he loves give birth can make the strongest man panic. How far apart are the contractions?"

Mariela swiped her damp hair away from her face. "Two minutes."

"When did you go into labor?"

"About two hours ago," she answered.

"Paulo took a long time," Diego remarked.

"This one is impatient." Already the strain showed on her face.

Diego handed candles and a small matchbook to Caroline. "Put these on the nightstands and light them."

Caroline frowned. One look at Diego stilled her protest. "All right."

"Thank you for taking a look at Ramón's father," Mariela said to her, voice tight.

Caroline watched pain sweep over Mariela's face. "You're welcome." She stirred herself to do as Diego asked, even as she wondered why Mariela was still standing. She shot a look at Diego, but his attention was focused on Mariela.

"Let me examine you," he said. "Lie down for a minute." He took her arm and led her toward the bed.

Mariela leaned on him, her jaw tight. "You'd think this would get easier." Her forehead glistened with sweat.

"Now is about the right time for you to begin cursing men in general."

Her lips quirked faintly. "Forget general. This is

as personal as it gets. I'm waiting for Ramón to come back in here so I can blister his ears."

Caroline didn't know how Mariela could joke when every line of her body was tense with pain. She dragged her attention away and concentrated on lighting the candles that seemed so superfluous.

Diego eased Mariela onto her back, then conducted an examination. "You're about ready. Feel the need to push yet?"

This time there was no teasing as Mariela's breathing grew strained. "I'm going to wait for Ramón."

"Let's hope the child will cooperate." Diego smiled. "Check her vitals, will you?" he said to Caroline, handing her a stethoscope.

Startled, still she reached for the instrument automatically, rightness settling into her bones when she clasped it. So long. It had been so long.

Her fingers fumbled slightly as she adapted to using her left hand. She glanced at her watch and counted. Lifting her head, she started to report to Diego, then realized he was kneeling before the altar in the corner of the room.

His head was bowed; his lips moved without sound. Fingers curled around a rosary, he pressed a kiss to the beads, then crossed himself and rose.

Rapt, Caroline watched him. Felt the power that exuded from him in waves. In that moment, he was larger than life, every bit a healer. A champion. She couldn't tear her gaze away.

Those seer's eyes locked on hers, and everything inside her stilled.

Then Mariela gripped the hand that held the stethoscope and squeezed.

And Ramón walked through the door.

Caroline blinked. Diego's gaze shifted to his patient.

He was a natural, she realized. Perhaps he had been a warrior, but within him also lay a man who fought death and suffering, who would battle on behalf of those the world ignored. A man of honor and compassion who answered the call, not of fame as Judd Carter craved, but of people who'd been forgotten by a world where profit mattered more than caring.

She didn't understand some of the methods he used. Wasn't sure she ever would.

But she recognized the calling, understood how it felt—that inner chord that resonated, deep and true, when who you were and what you could do mattered. When you forgot about the world where you needed to pay bills or fought for prestige or advancement.

She'd experienced the pure moments when she'd held a life in her hands, cradled a beating heart in her palm and made the difference. Brought someone's husband back, restored a mother to her family.

At those times, she, too, had known the breath of holiness. Understood that life could be more than simply survival.

"Caroline." Diego handed her a set of gloves to match his, and she snapped out of her reverie.

"Why are you—" She gestured with the gloves. "I can't—my hand—"

"Forget what you can't do," he said. "Let's see what you can."

Anticipation rose in her like strong wine, rich and heady. She didn't hold back the smile as she met his gaze. "All right." She nodded, working the gloves on, if not with her usual verve. "All right."

The pride in his eyes warmed her. "Good." He turned to Mariela, sheltered now against Ramón's chest, her hands gripping his hard. "Ready, *mamacita? Vamos a dar a luz.*"

Mariela tried to smile, but another pain had her in its grip. "This is the last one, Ramón Vargas, do you hear me?"

Ramón kept his voice light even as his dark eyes glittered with worry. "You say that every time, *querida.*"

"But this time I mean it." She grunted. "*Madre de Dios,* it hurts—" she cried out. "I have to push, Diego."

Diego knelt with haste, and Caroline wondered at the cost to his hip. "*Soy listo, mamacita.* Let's bring this little one into the world."

Caroline couldn't help creeping closer, despite the knowledge that she could do little to help. She wasn't really needed here, but the room swirled with fierce concentration and joy and love.

The head appeared, cradled in Diego's big hands. "You're doing very well," he soothed. "One more push, Mariela."

Caroline spared a glance at the woman, fierce in her determination, her face glowing with purpose. Ramón gripped her torso in his arms, murmuring to her, his own face alight with so much love Caroline had to look away.

The baby slipped out and into Diego's hands. "It's a boy!" he exclaimed. "Suction, please," he said over his shoulder. Caroline grasped the bulb and moved forward, hearing Mariela's cry of triumph and Ramón's muttered prayers.

"Here," said Diego. "Hold his head."

"I can't—"

"I'll hold his body." With swift grace, he plucked the suction bulb from her and cleared the infant's nostrils.

Terrified because the child was so fragile, Caroline added her damaged hand to the good one, holding the slippery, wet head with none of the assurance with which she'd once held human hearts.

Gently, Diego rubbed the baby's chest. The little boy's mouth opened in a lusty cry.

"Ay, m'ijo," Ramón shouted.

"Let me see him," Mariela insisted.

Diego made the sign of the cross over the child's forehead and murmured over him in Spanish. The only word Caroline recognized was *tesoro*.

Treasure.

She cradled the tiny head in her hand. "It's a miracle," she whispered, staring into the baby's eyes.

"Every time," Diego agreed. He slid his hand under hers and started to rise.

So warm. His hands always seemed unusually warm.

For a second, his balance faltered as his hip balked.

"Let me help." Caroline relinquished her hold on the infant's head to Diego and placed her good hand under his elbow to assist him.

He shot her a glance. Jaw tight, he nodded. "Thanks."

Pride. He didn't give himself credit for all he'd overcome. Didn't allow imperfection in himself.

He placed the baby in Mariela's arms, then returned to deliver the placenta. "Hand me that blue bowl." He gestured to the pottery nestled inside a box in the bag he'd brought with him.

Frowning, she handed it to him, watching as he slid the placenta into the bowl. "Shouldn't you be clamping off the umbilical cord?"

"Let it stop pulsing first. Pass me the string and scissors, please."

She complied, her gaze darting from the blue bowl to the family so absorbed in their little miracle.

Diego's gaze followed hers. "It is our custom to bury the placenta, to feed back to the earth so that the cycle will not die."

She detected a slight stiffness in the set of his shoulders, as if he expected her to argue or poke fun. But she was still wrapped in the spell of holding that tiny head, of watching a new life begin. She caught his gaze. "I think that's lovely. We've drifted far away, haven't we, in the modern world?" She grappled for the right words. "In a hospital, it's just...waste. Or research material. But here..."

His eyes softened. "Here, we must be closer to the earth. To the past." His mouth quirked. "But not so far that I don't check the Apgar scale. He's a perfect ten, would you agree?"

Caroline scrambled to remember the Apgar scale. Points were given for breathing, for color, for movement, but— She smiled. "I think so, but I'd admit to being a little rusty on it."

Diego recited the scale for her.

"Delivered a lot of babies in the military, did you?" she teased.

Something sad ghosted across his face. "A few," he admitted. "But seldom so healthy. And never in peace." He turned away before she could ask more.

With efficiency, he tied off the cord and handed scissors to Ramón, who bowed his head, held Mariela's hand and prayed, then cut the cord. Giving the scissors back to Diego, he settled again on the bed, this time beside his wife. She handed him the baby, and the expression on Ramón's face made Caroline's eyes sting.

"Carlos," Ramón said, glancing at Mariela, who nodded. Then he regarded Caroline. "The closest we can come to Caroline for a boy's name."

Her jaw dropped. "But—" She tried again. "What about Diego?"

"Already done. Our second is named after *mi compadre* here."

"But I—"

A look from Diego warned her.

Caroline stopped long enough for it to sink in. To realize how much it mattered. "Thank you," she managed. "I'm very honored."

"Good, then. It's settled." Ramón rose. "Come with me, *hijo*. Let's get you cleaned up before you start yelling for food."

Diego clapped his friend on the back. "I'll follow you."

Which left Caroline alone with Mariela, not sure what to do. "Can I—would you like to clean up some?"

Hair matted with sweat, face drained with the effort, the new mother smiled. "It's all right. Don't worry about it. I can wait until Elena comes. I'm sure your hospital has others to do such things.''

Of course it did. But she wasn't at Mercy, and if she were in this woman's position, she'd want to change her gown and have clean sheets and all that. ''Just tell me where the linens are and point me toward the bathroom.''

Mariela nodded. ''To the right in the hall. Thank you.''

Caroline headed for the door.

''Doctora,'' Mariela said. ''I'm glad you were here.''

Caroline stopped. The wonder of it all rose within her again. She smiled at the woman whose face glowed with a tired happiness. ''Me, too.''

And realized that she really meant it.

CHAPTER NINE

"I'LL DROP YOU OFF at the cabin before I head back," Diego said an hour later, after they'd celebrated with the new parents and been toasted by the extended family, who were still arriving in droves.

"Go back where?"

"I have to finish hanging the Sheetrock. Get some of it taped and floated, too, if I'm lucky." The high of the delivery and celebration were fading. Reality crowded in, exhaustion close on its heels.

Caroline studied him. "Aren't you worn-out?"

He shrugged. It didn't matter if he was.

"Why don't you ask them for help?" She indicated the house behind them. "They'd give you anything right now."

"I know they would."

Her unflinching regard made him shift on the seat. "You're like Lobo," she said softly. "But I don't understand why. Everyone here loves you. Practically worships the ground you walk on."

He glanced away. "I—that's not—" He gave up.

Trying to explain ventured onto paths he didn't want to tread.

Her considering gaze didn't abate. "Why?"

He cursed inwardly, willing her to drop the subject. "Why what?"

"Why does that bother you?"

Diego's fingers stilled on the ignition key. "It doesn't matter."

She was silent for a moment. "You're lying."

He whipped his head around. "You don't—" He looked forward again, jaw clenched, then put the trunk in gear and began to dirve. "Do you want a ride to your cabin or not?"

One hand touched his arm softly. The feel of it burned his skin. "What happened when you were injured?"

Diego closed his eyes. Wished she would go away. "It's not something I talk about."

Her hand drew back, taking its warmth with her. "All right."

The slight tremor in her voice made him feel like a jerk. He exhaled in a gust. "I don't need my head shrunk. Things happened, that's all. Things I wish—" His throat tightened.

"I've made mistakes, too, you know." Her voice almost convinced him that she could understand. "There was this woman who should have lived to be ninety. She was barely fifty, had a husband who adored her and kids and grandkids. I'd lost cases before, but never one this personal." She looked at him then, and the misery in her eyes told the tale. "She gave me a chance when I was green. Chose me over a colleague with more experience. She trusted me with her life and—" Caroline averted her face. "He might have saved her. Probably would have. Instead, I had to walk out there and tell her family that what should have been a simple surgery hadn't worked. I'd told her—told them all—that it was a no-brainer, and instead she died on the table."

That the loss still dug spurs into her was evident. "Medicine isn't a perfect science, Caroline."

She lifted agonized eyes to his. "I know." Her stare didn't waver. "But it doesn't make it hurt less. People depend on us, and sometimes we don't measure up."

The arrow, however unintended, hit its mark.

He pulled to a stop in front of her cabin. The vision that never fully left him bloomed again: Townsend's eyes begging Diego to save him, even though his femoral artery had been severed, his right leg turned to hamburger.

"Diego." Caroline's voice jerked him out of memory. "Talk to me. I've seen things no one should have to. Maybe others here wouldn't understand, but I do."

And finally, after three years, he couldn't jam the door closed any longer.

"The mission where I was—" He gestured toward his bad hip. "It was bad."

She waited for him to continue. When he didn't, she prompted. "You lost men?"

After a long pause, he nodded. "Two." Bitter regret rose again. "Two out of six, goddamn it." Rage shot past it, stronger for being forced from the light for so long. "Townsend was just a kid, the new guy on the squad. His wife was pregnant with their first child—" He stared straight ahead, swallowing hard. "The squad depended on me to patch them up, send them all home in one piece. I always managed it. Sometimes by the skin of my teeth, but every one of them had made it home before. Every single time. Until Bosnia."

"So what happened?" Her voice was soft but intent, as though she wouldn't stop until she'd drawn off the poison.

Diego felt the rising of something black and putrid, something he wanted to bury so deep that maybe one day it would quit scoring him with merciless claws. "It doesn't matter," he snapped.

He thought she'd take the easy way out. He was offering her what she'd said she wanted: no involvement with any of them, the acknowledgment that she was only here for a short time.

Instead, she rose to her knees on the seat, hands on her thighs, facing him. "You might be able to fool the others, but you can't fool me. I've watched people die in my care. I know how it feels." She touched one fist to her heart. "I haven't been in combat, but I understand that every single life you lose takes something away that you never get back. It doesn't even have to be your fault. A healer is a fighter. We don't want to lose—and every time we do, it kills something inside us."

A malevolent pressure crowded his chest, pushed so hard he couldn't breathe. He grabbed the door handle and burst out of the truck, head swiveling from side to side like an animal seeking refuge when survival was at stake.

Caroline rounded the cab of the pickup, placing herself in his path. "Talk to me," she urged, one hand pressing against the center of his chest, where fury and misery and heartache slammed together until he thought he would explode.

"No," he shouted. "Leave me the hell alone." He whirled away and started to run, but his hip chose that moment to collapse. He fell to his knees on the ground.

His body bowed beneath the weight of anger and sorrow and the pain that never left him. He dug his fingers into his hair, and pain burst forth like razors flaying his skin.

Caroline's arms slid around his shoulders.

He resisted. Fighting what he needed too much. What he didn't deserve.

One hand pressed his head into her breasts, and

she murmured into his ears words he couldn't make out, but the sound of them soothed him, reached out to him through the tearing pain, the roaring maelstrom.

He'd never expected a lifeline, not from this too-thin woman living on nerves. She comforted him as he would never have allowed his family to do. Somehow knowing that she'd been in that position, that she understood how it felt to have another human being's life in her hands and be unable to save him, reached down inside where he'd been alone for so long.

"We shouldn't have been there," he confessed. "It was my fault. I was worried about a group of children. I wanted to make sure they were safe. My team wouldn't let me go alone. It turned out to be a setup. An extremist group didn't want Muslim kids tainted by contact with The Great Satan."

"You didn't know."

"But I had no business trying to be anyone's savior. My team trusted me. They—" His voice faltered. "They teased me about being a romantic, always checking out the local healing traditions. Whatever country we were in, they'd bring things back to me—plants, stories…"

He shoved away. Rose unsteadily. "I got them killed—Townsend and Martin. I almost got everyone killed."

She touched his shoulder. "You nearly died, too."

He shrugged off her hand. Whirled toward her. "You think that helps?"

She stood her ground. "Nothing helps but time—and forgiving yourself for surviving." She cocked her head. "Clinging to the pain is easy, Diego. It's going on that's hard. You feel guilty that you're alive and they're not, but—"

"Get out," he raged. "Get away from me. Just—"

"No." Into the darkness swallowing him, she stepped, a pale flame. "I'm not going anywhere."

"Damn you—" He grabbed for her, hating that he'd bared his soul to her, stripped himself down to the bone. Desperate to stop her from looking so deep inside him, he dug his fingers into her hair and dragged her against him, seizing her mouth in a kiss meant to distract. To defend.

He didn't know what response he'd expected. Maybe she'd slap him. Maybe she'd draw back, remind him that she was a hotshot surgeon and he was some sort of mongrel. Less.

Instead she cradled his cheek tenderly and let herself go, turning to fire in his arms. Answering his fury as if she needed him as much as, right then, he needed her.

When she trembled, he murmured, "I won't hurt you."

"You will. You can't help it," she said with certainty. "But right now I don't care."

He couldn't think straight enough to argue. "If you don't want me to take you on this hard ground, you'd better walk away now." What he wouldn't give to sweep her up in his arms the way he once would have done with ease.

Somehow they made it to her porch, Diego half carrying her, Caroline's fingers ranging over his body, clawing and digging in…stroking and petting until he thought he'd lose his mind.

He'd been careful for so long. Afraid to let the beast loose for fear of whom he would hurt. Once more he grasped for a leash to jerk it back.

Caroline wouldn't let him. She all but crawled up his body on her front porch.

"Caroline, don't—"

She actually growled at him. Then her fingers fumbled at the buttons on his shirt. "I want to see you," she muttered. "I have to touch you." She held her head back, eyes filled with challenge. "I want those hands on me. God, I love your hands. They're the sexiest things I've ever seen."

"I've got scars," he warned. "Terrible ones."

"You're talking to a person who makes scars for a living." She smiled, and his heart dropped out of his chest. "They don't scare me. You afraid of me, Diego?"

Incredible. Somehow, she'd transformed his

shame and agony into a dare. He searched for the place in his chest that had been filled with darkness for three years and couldn't find it.

Yet part of him clung to the guilt that had been his constant companion.

"Are you?" She challenged him again.

It couldn't be this easy to let go. He still had to pay, all his life he would pay for—

Caroline wrapped one leg around his thigh and rocked her pelvis against him—

Every last thought in his head vanished.

Diego dove into her, gripping her hair in one hand, wrapping her so tightly in his arms that he wasn't sure either one of them would ever breathe again. He expected her to protest— Instead, she laughed, the raunchiest, most seductive laugh he'd ever heard from a woman.

And in that moment, he wanted to laugh, too. The relief of it broke past all the barriers he'd carefully constructed to protect everyone he loved from the darkness that had swallowed him whole.

"That's it," he muttered, backing her toward the cabin door.

"God, I hope so," she sighed, her mouth curving against his lips. When he would have urged her toward the bedroom, instead she drew him down to the floor.

Then she rose over him and pressed her lips to

the opening of his shirt, licking the spot above his collarbone and making the hair rise on his arms.

"We should—" he gasped.

Caroline settled herself over him, wiggling to maximum effect. "I don't take orders well, Diego. Anyone at Mercy could tell you that I'm used to being the one who hands them out." She brushed against him again and smiled. "Why don't you just relax and forget that you're used to giving them, too."

For a moment, he could only lie there and stare at her, green eyes alight with mischief and humor, devoid of all the anger and sorrow they'd held since the first day she'd ordered the caretaker to grab her bags. "You'd like that, wouldn't you?" he asked.

She smiled. "I'd like most anything that got you naked. I've been thinking about you without your clothes."

He gritted his teeth. "Don't say that." He closed his eyes. "I haven't been with a woman since—"

Her eyes widened. Her smile followed. "Well...I'm a little rusty myself, but it hasn't been three years. You should definitely let me take the lead." She winked at him. "Just until you get the hang of it."

Diego laughed out loud, and the sound of it was odd to his own ears. When was the last time he'd laughed, belly deep?

She was amazing, this woman who straddled him now, wiggling until he feared he'd explode.

Faster than she could react, he flipped them. Eyes wide in shock, she opened her mouth but nothing came out.

He laughed again but heard the roughness in his throat. He wasn't going to last long this time.

This time. With that, Diego acknowledged that there would be a next time, insane as it was to even consider such a thing.

Then Caroline slid her tongue around her lips in a slow sweep so carnal it shot his pulse into the danger zone.

Then she followed it up by using her good hand to unbuckle his belt and work at the button on the top of his jeans.

"Sweet—" He all but leaped off her. "Stop that."

"No," said the woman who'd battled the big boys and won, who knows how many times.

"Don't." He grabbed her hands and stilled them as his heart raced. "I can't—" He swallowed hard. "I'm too ready. We have to slow down."

A protest sprang to her lips until she looked into his eyes. She glanced away, and he realized that for all her bluster, she was as uncertain as he was.

Two damaged bodies. Two tenuous hearts.

A premonition shook Diego to his marrow. Something was different this time. With this woman. His heart would not escape without harm; somehow he sensed it.

Would she feel it? Did she already? Was that why she pushed to make it physical and quick?

"Caroline," he began. "This is important."

She shook her head and refused to meet his gaze. "It's just sex."

"You're wrong." He knew too little about her and might not like what he learned. She would definitely not like what she learned about him.

But she was still wrong.

Her head shook slowly from side to side. He clasped her jaw and tilted her face toward him.

Tear-bright eyes greeted his. "It can't be important," she whispered. "I have to leave soon."

No, he wanted to shout. Wanted to demand. He didn't know what they had between them, but surely she could see it wasn't casual, wasn't something to be flippant about.

Why? he asked the void. Why her?

You could go with her, a little voice murmured. *It's the world you always wanted. The life you planned.*

He sank to the side, separating their bodies. Within him, memory stirred. For a moment, he ignored that he was damaged, that his grandmother needed him, that so many people depended on him. Wanted him to be something he wasn't.

Instead, he let himself linger in the dreams he'd

once had. Let them become new dreams, where he fit into Caroline's world, where he was once again free—

Bitter longing twisted inside him that she could go back and he never could. That she belonged and he never would.

He had to stop now. Maybe she could be casual about this, but it wasn't in him. Better to remain alone.

In his mind's eye rose the faces of those he loved here, those who depended on him, who believed in him. He couldn't leave, even if Caroline wanted him.

And she wouldn't stay.

Awkwardly, he pushed himself to his feet. "I'd better go," he said.

"Wait," she called out. "Diego—"

"I can't." He didn't look back as he stumbled through her front door and out to his pickup. He avoided his rearview mirror for fear of what he'd see.

If only he could forget what he'd just lost.

He didn't return to the clinic as he'd intended. Tonight his will was not up to the task of prevailing, not this time.

He considered seeking out his grandmother but rejected it out of hand. She'd comfort him, yes. She might even understand what he couldn't yet grasp himself.

But he couldn't take the chance that she'd see how tempted he was to leave this place. How Caroline had dredged up yearnings he'd thought long dead and buried.

So instead, he drove back to his place and parked the truck. Lobo brushed against his legs, whimpering, but Diego barely paused to scratch his head.

"Not now, buddy," he said. "Let me be."

Alone, he headed for his spring, the place he'd passed many an endless night, searching for peace.

As THE SOUND of his pickup died away, Caroline rolled over on the floor and curled into a tight ball.

If she let herself think about what had happened, she'd scream. Or claw. Or break something or—

Damn him. How could he abandon her like this? How could he turn away from what she'd offered—

But she knew without asking, really. There was no trick to it at all; hadn't she known that?

She was hard to love.

But easy to leave.

She shoved to sitting, jerked her head high. Screw him. He was nothing to her, a man hiding out in the back of beyond, too afraid of his past mistakes to try again, to take the leap—

But even as the uncharitable thoughts bloomed like poisonous flowers, shame assailed her.

It wasn't that simple.

He was far from that simple. He'd hurt her pride,

yes. Scared her by how much he could make her want him. Terrified her with the need she'd felt, the way he'd refused to let it be just basic sex and opened her, for a moment, to a breathless vista of more, of possibilities that called out to a part of her she'd thought long dead.

She scrambled to her feet. Headed for her bedroom and yanked a suitcase from the closet. Opened it on the bed and whirled toward the bureau—

And remembered that she had no way to leave, not tonight. She was over two hours from the nearest airport and had no way to get there, anyway.

Elena. Would Elena take her? Without asking questions?

No.

Ramón was with his wife and kids and new baby. Adelaida didn't drive.

She slapped the suitcase closed and began to pace. In the morning, she would call Sam and force him to order her a car and driver. She could be out of here by noon.

Okay. She would go ahead and pack. Be ready to take off.

Her gaze drifted to the quilt she'd bought from Elena; her thoughts returned to the miracle of Mariela's child.

Then she considered Adelaida and how she'd explain to her why she was leaving. *Something came up. A patient needs me.*

But Trini Vargas needed her, too. The equipment could be here any day.

Damn you, Diego. You've made me care. I don't want to. I have to go back. I don't belong here.

She remembered the devastation in his eyes. Recalled how much she'd wanted him. Craved him. Wanted to lose herself in his arms.

It's important, he'd insisted.

It can't be, Diego.

She couldn't let it.

CHAPTER TEN

BUT IN THE MORNING, Sam couldn't be reached. Off at a conference, his assistant said. Caroline had insisted that she try. She knew him; he was never totally out of contact.

Sam's assistant would not agree to hire a car and driver; she would consent to giving Sam the message when he called in. No taxi would come two and a half hours from El Paso.

Caroline kicked the couch and slammed down her phone. All she'd gotten for her effort was sore toes.

She grabbed up her mug of tea and stomped out to the porch. For a few moments, she saw nothing, blinded by frustration.

But slowly the vista settled in; the peace of this place eased her breathing back from a huff. She heard the mockingbird that seemed to have taken up residence in the tree a few feet from the porch. In the distance, she heard cattle. When she looked to her right, she saw the rapidly growing foal race past his mother.

Caroline drew in a deep breath and smiled. What

was it about this place, so different from anything she'd known? The air hadn't yet heated too much; the wind blew her frustration away. Once more, something deep inside her settled.

Movement off the porch caught her gaze. When she saw what it was, everything in her stilled.

Lobo.

She glanced around for Dulcita, but the old dog was nowhere to be found. The two of them came her way often now, but never Lobo by himself.

Almost afraid to breathe for fear of scaring him off, Caroline sank slowly to the porch steps.

Lobo halted, but he didn't run away. Instead, he watched her with wary eyes, his entire body rigid.

He made her think of Diego. For precious moments last night, Diego had trusted her. Had let her close.

Had accepted comfort that was so unlike her to give. Doing so had opened something new inside her, had weakened walls she'd counted on for years.

With that weakening had come hunger—roaring, clawing, desperate to be filled. The remembered power of it could make her shudder still.

She had wanted him badly. And not just for sex, no matter what she'd said. If he hadn't torn himself away, no telling what kind of mistake she would have made.

"Where is he, Lobo?" she murmured. "What did he do last night?"

Lobo cocked his head, an almost human intelligence in his eyes.

"You love him, don't you?" She extended her hand. "He loves you, too."

It was her damaged hand she held out, and soon the arm trembled, once her strongest but too long unused and now turned weak.

Just as she was about to drop it, Lobo moved. He crouched, edging forward only a pace or two, but the thrill of it sang through her. She braced her right arm with her left hand and gritted her teeth to hold on. "That's right, fella. I won't hurt you, I swear."

Lobo eased a few feet closer.

"You're such a handsome guy...come on."

He was within three feet of her; the muscles of her arm screamed, but she held still. "Come on, boy. It'll be okay," she crooned.

Two feet. One foot. He stopped.

Caroline extended her fingers, palm up, and bent forward with exquisite care. "Aren't you the most beautiful thing?" Perhaps two inches separated them now. She held her breath.

His nostrils flared as he drew in her scent, ears high and alert, body singing with tension.

She was afraid to speak. Slowly...very slowly, she leaned.

One finger touched his muzzle. He didn't run.

Lobo's wolf-yellow eyes caught hers and held.

Caroline had the oddest sense they had a message there for her, if only she could make it out.

So much like his master he was. Strong but so alone. Afraid to let himself be loved.

Love. The very word shook her hard.

And Lobo bounded off, disappearing around the porch.

Caroline's arm gave way. She dropped her head to her knees.

AFTER A WHILE, she couldn't stand her own company anymore. She tucked her cell phone in her pocket, put on her hat and strode out the door toward town.

Outside Adelaida's gate, she paused, wanting more than was rational to invite herself inside.

But the old woman saw too much, and Caroline was too raw. So she kept walking.

When she arrived at Ramón's store, chaos reigned. Elena stood at the cash register, casting glances toward her kitchen and muttering Spanish in tones that had Caroline betting the words weren't polite.

"Come here—" Elena ordered. "Do you want to run the cash register or cook?"

Caroline jolted. "What?"

"Don't be slow, girlfriend. I don't have time. Ramón and Mariela are sleeping in, and for *Dios* knows what reason, I told him to stay home today.

I can't be in two places at once and—'' She let out a shriek. ''My *frijoles*—they're burning—''

Before Caroline could blink, Elena had shoved her behind the cash register and taken off at a run.

''But I've never—''

Elena was already too far away.

The old woman standing patiently on the other side of the counter smiled softly. A rapid stream of Spanish ensued as she gestured toward the small stack of groceries.

''I don't—I can't—'' Caroline dug back in memory to high school. *''No hablo español,''* she said.

The old woman lifted one palm and shrugged. *''No hablo inglés.''* But she smiled as though they were boon companions.

Caroline glanced at the ancient cash register and attempted to decipher its keys. Then she looked at the groceries for price tags, but there were none.

Elena's colorful curses split the air.

The old woman grinned.

Caroline grinned back. ''All right,'' she said. ''Let's see what we've got.''

The transaction required trips back and forth from the shelves and more than a little sign language, but between the two of them, Caroline and her first customer came to what she sincerely hoped was the correct total. She helped the old woman out the door, ridiculously proud of the few words of Spanish she'd dragged out of the far reaches of her brain, as well as the fact that she'd been able to push a few keys with her right index finger without her wrist brace and twice released her grip on cans without using the other hand to pry them out.

Elena was still muttering when she returned. "So would you like a job?" she asked.

"You'd better let me run through what I did before you take that step." Caroline explained; Elena had only a few corrections to make.

"Why aren't the prices marked on the groceries?" Caroline asked.

Elena shrugged. "Ramón is always here and he knows them by heart."

"That was nice of you to offer to help him out so he could stay home today."

"Well, my brother is a pain in the neck, but oh, that little Carlito—don't you just want to eat him up?"

Caroline had never been all that interested in babies before, but she'd never forget the feel of that tiny head. "He's beautiful." Her fingers tingled with the memory of the precious weight, of Diego's fingers beneath hers.

"So are you here to help Diego today?"

Caroline jolted. "No—I can't—I'm going to—" She frowned. "Where is he?"

"Checking on Carlito, seeing someone who can't make it in—who knows?" Elena leaned closer. "I think he's going to be very busy today."

"Why?"

"Because—" Elena's eyes danced. "Everyone is working together to keep the party a surprise."

"Party?"

"It's Diego's birthday. Tonight we celebrate, if only—ah!" she exclaimed. "You! You're the answer."

"To what?"

"You have to stay with him. Keep him here as much as you can, but if he must leave, keep him away from Adelaida's."

"Me?"

"You're the only one, don't you see that? You have the perfect excuse."

"But I can't—" What if Sam called? She was leaving today and—

"It's important. The entire village is coming together to celebrate. Everyone wants to thank Diego for all he's done. For what he means to us and to our future." Her dark eyes turned serious. "We need him. Mama Lalita grows old, and for so long we all worried. But now Diego is here. He will take her place. He will save us."

Caroline thought of the weight Diego carried already—the guilt and pain, the physical cost to him. Added to the burden of the past were the hopes and needs of his people. Few men could shoulder the load; she knew Diego would never drop it. The villagers were in good hands.

But what would it cost Diego?

"Elena—" She almost launched into an argument, but it was not her place.

Elena breezed on. "Mama Lalita had offered to accompany him, but he's so protective of her that he wouldn't agree. His mother said she would try, but he'd never fall for it. We didn't know what we were going to do, but now you—"

"His mother? Will she be here?"

"Of course. His entire family will. Jesse is coming from Washington, and Zane intends to fly in from location, though he'll have to fly back out tonight."

His entire family. Diego seemed so alone that though she'd heard about them, they didn't seem real. "Where will they stay?"

"Oh, they'll probably go back to Alpine. Jenna has school, Jesse and Zane have to return to work and Hal MacAllister swears he can only sleep in his own bed. It's just fifty miles back to their house." Excitement vibrated the air around Elena. "So will you do it? Will you help?"

How could she spend the day with him after last night? "I don't know if he'll let me."

Elena's eyes dripped pity. "*Mujer,* the day a woman can't convince a man to take her where she wants to go…bite your tongue. Of course he'll let you. Hasn't he been wanting you to help?"

"But—" Last night. She would never share it with anyone. It was too private.

Elena was right. He had invited her more than once. But that was before she'd all but thrown him to the ground and—

"You don't know what you're asking."

Dark eyebrows arched. Then Elena's eyes narrowed. "What's happened between you two?"

"Nothing," Caroline said too quickly.

The door opened, and Diego stepped inside.

"Showtime," Elena hissed. "Don't let us down." Then she turned, smile bright and wide. *"Buenas días,* Diego."

He smiled in answer. Then he saw Caroline, and the smile faded.

The silence was deafening.

"Coward," Elena spat, then her voice rose. "I have excellent news for you, *compadre. La doctora* has decided to accompany you on your rounds. Paulo Aguirre just called, and his eldest daughter's stomach hurts." She pushed Caroline in front of her. "Paulo's truck is acting up, and he wondered if you could come there instead." In Caroline's ear, she whispered. "We need until four o'clock."

Here's your hat—what's your hurry? Before either of them could protest, Caroline and Diego found themselves outside, heading for his truck.

SHE WAS GOOD. She hadn't given herself enough credit, Diego thought. Watching Caroline Malone become a doctor again had compensated for the awkward silences whenever they veered from the subject of patient care.

She'd been all nerves at first, hanging back, dodging any real contact with the patients. But it hadn't been long before she started asking questions, then firing off opinions like rounds of ammo. If there hadn't been a language barrier, she might have taken over completely.

She loved it; he could see that. Practicing medicine made her seem both wise and young. Despite the limitations of her injured hand, her moves were sure and smooth, her concentration intense, her mind quick to grasp nuances and find solutions. Even with the limitations of his supplies and equipment, she found ways to circumvent them.

And all the while, her eyes sparkled. Her frame straightened. Pride reemerged and joy surfaced. At the moment, she looked all of sixteen.

"Why did we get away from house calls?" she mused. "You learn so much seeing the patient at home."

"Tough to do surgery in the kitchen," he said. "Mortality rates aren't pretty."

She answered his grin. "But homes don't have the nasty infections that only live in hospitals." She studied him. "You had to do field surgery, didn't you?"

He nodded.

"How? How could you ever—" Her hands rose, palms up. "I try to subtract all the benefits I'm accustomed to having in the O.R., but I just can't imagine what it's like."

"You do what you have to." He shrugged. "Every man carries an IV kit and bag of saline on him when he goes into a mission. The medic carries his own pack loaded with all the essentials."

"What do you do if there's fighting?"

"First you secure the area. If there's gunfire, you return it. Then you get to work on stabilizing the patient."

"So you have the same weapons training as the rest of them?"

He nodded. "You're Special Forces first, then a medic. You have to be able to fight."

"Was it hard?" she asked softly. "To have to kill?"

He didn't answer at first.

"I'm sorry," she said. "I have no right—"

"Yes." He cut her off. "It's hard. It goes against your instinct to heal, but you can't think about that. Your team is all that matters. Protecting them, caring for them…you do whatever it takes to ensure that they survive."

The silence around them thickened. He thought about last night again, not that it had ever been far from his mind.

"Forget I asked," she said. "It's none of my business."

"You're right." He glanced over at her, not sure he was ready to make the admission. "But...at least you know how it feels to—" He looked away.

"To lose someone?" she asked. "Someone you're supposed to save?"

Diego stared out the windshield, jaw tight. "Yeah."

"It's not fair," she murmured. "They expect too much of you."

He blinked. "What?"

"Healing and fighting are poles apart. I don't know how you survived it."

He looked over, and her green eyes fastened on his. For a moment, he couldn't speak. When she looked too deeply, it weakened him. He couldn't afford that.

Her empathy was almost more than he could take. He wanted to grab her, hold her tight. Wanted to run far and fast to a refuge where those too-seeing eyes couldn't reach. But what he'd comprehended last night hadn't changed. Their paths were different.

"You are an amazing man, Diego Montalvo."

He stared. "What?"

"You've taken something most people wouldn't survive and turned it around. Made something horrible into something good."

"You're wrong." He clenched his jaw. "You don't understand."

"I think I do," she said quietly. "But the need of this valley weighs on you, doesn't it? Gratitude is a heavy burden."

He couldn't breathe. "I have to help Mama Lalita. I owe her."

"She wouldn't ask if she knew how much it hurt you."

No, she wouldn't. But that didn't change anything. "I walked away from here. I rejected these people who never harmed me. My father's people." He swallowed. "It would have pained him deeply."

"If he was anything like your grandmother, he would have understood. He would have wanted the best for you."

His head whipped around. "You don't get it. You don't know what it's like not to belong anywhere, to have people on both sides who care about you but don't have the faintest notion that you're caught between them and—" He shook his head. "Never mind."

"I've never been split between two cultures, no," she acknowledged. "But I do understand what it's like not to belong anywhere."

How could she, in her privileged world? "Tell me."

She hesitated, cocking her head to study him. She must have seen what she needed because she nodded. "All right." Slow and halting at first, her story picked up its pace, and he understood at last why she was so solitary. So afraid to trust.

"You should search for your sisters."

She looked startled. "I tried once but found no trace." She stared out the side window, but he could see the vulnerability in the line of her jaw. "They've probably gone on without me. I've contacted a private investigator to try again, but I wonder if I might only upset things." A faint smile curved her lips. "Ivy is probably married with a house full of babies by now. That's all she ever really wanted—to take care of people." Her eyelashes blinked rapidly. "She tried to convince the social workers that she and I could take care of Chloe by ourselves."

He heard the catch in her voice. "Did you want to try?"

Her lids lowered. "It didn't matter. There was no way they were turning a four-year-old over to two teenagers. I tried to tell Ivy that—" Her head dipped.

With both hands, she scrubbed her face. "God— if I live to be a hundred, I'll never forget how Ivy sobbed in my arms, like the world was ending. Then—" She faltered.

He could imagine the rest. "Then they separated you."

Her blond hair shielded her from his vision. "They wouldn't even let me call her," she whispered. ''They said maybe in a month or two, but by then I was in the next place because I was too much trouble and—''

He waited for her to continue, but she didn't. ''I was lucky that my mom was so strong. Then there were Mama Lalita and the others in the village who helped out until my mother met Hal.''

She brushed at her eyes. ''My mother wasn't strong. After that bastard left us, she just…folded. As if she was nothing without him.'' Her voice turned harsh. ''I'll never forgive her for that.''

But he heard the pain and the fear. ''You're nothing like her, Caroline.''

Her head swiveled, her eyes bright with fury and resolution. ''Damn right, I'm not. I'll never let a man do that to me.''

In that moment, Diego thought he understood why she'd insisted that the attraction between them be relegated to just sex. Mere physical attraction was manageable. You could ignore appetites of the flesh, could wrestle them into submission.

The heart's hungers were a tougher task. Not so easily ignored.

Or satisfied.

If he was wise, he'd agree to her terms. She had wounds as deep as his own and a life that put her far out of his reach. Until or unless she was forced to accept that she could never return to the surgical suite where she defined herself, they might as well live planets apart. There was no future in getting involved with her. Already things had gone too far.

But still something inside him rebelled. What he and she understood about each other was not something to cast away or scoff at.

Neither were the differences between them.

Yet again Diego rammed headfirst into the cold, hard fact that his life was here and hers was not. Would never be, as long as she could hold out hope of recovery.

And God knows he would never wish hopelessness on anyone. Especially a woman he had come to admire and respect.

And want. Beyond all reason.

"You're wrong to cast all men in your father's light." Frustration made his voice sharper than he might wish in calmer moments. "Every marriage isn't one-sided. Yes, he left you, but she played a part."

"I wouldn't have stayed with her, either," Caroline vowed. "But that's no excuse for leaving my sisters. Ivy was always so easy, and he adored Chloe."

"What about you?"

Her shoulders stiffened. "That's different."

He frowned. "Why?"

She only shrugged.

Diego clasped her chin and turned her toward him. "Why, Caroline? Why shouldn't he have stayed for you, too?'' He felt her chin quiver. Saw her blinking hard against the moisture pooling in her eyes.

She jerked her chin from his grasp and averted her face, but not before he saw it crumple.

He pulled the truck off the road and shut off the engine, then placed one hand on her shoulder. ''You can't think he left because of you.''

She grappled for the door handle, but he was quicker, dragging her into his arms, feeling her body quiver under the force of her emotions.

''Tell me,'' he urged. ''Talk to me.'' Here was her poisoned wound that needed lancing.

Tension wound her tighter and tighter, but he held on.

Finally she broke. ''He—he—'' Her voice hitched. ''He wanted a boy. Always. I tried to show him that I could be as good as a son, but it didn't matter. Nothing I did ever—'' She slapped against Diego's hands, wriggling to get away. ''Let me go. I don't want you to—''

Diego forgot about his resolutions to stay away. Instead, he slid out from under the wheel and pulled her into his lap, cradling her within his arms. ''He was a fool,'' he murmured into her hair. ''He lost out on the best of his daughters.''

Finally the fight went out of her, and she sagged against his chest, sobbing her heart out.

Diego didn't move, even though his hip screamed

for relief. He pressed his lips to her hair and slid one hand up and down her spine, murmuring soothing words he knew she wasn't hearing.

When the storm of tears subsided, Caroline's body tensed as embarrassment caught her in its grip.

"No," he said. "It's too late for that, Caroline."

She relaxed slowly, her breath coming in halting half sobs until finally it eased.

Diego knew then that she was as open to him as she'd ever be. That he could seize the moment to turn her face to his and she'd welcome his kiss, his touch.

But he didn't want her grateful or weakened. He wanted Caroline to come to him with all the power and edgy vigor that was hers. Wanted her to crave him as he did her, with mind and body and a spirit that was as strong as any he'd ever encountered.

Wanted her to know it wasn't just sex, nor was it a need for simple kindness or respite.

Maybe he could even sway her to stay. Right now she needed him. Last night she'd made it clear she wanted him.

But to do so would be wrong, so Diego cast off what he wanted and did what was right for Caroline. Sliding one hand over her bright hair, he tilted her face to his and carefully kissed away her tears.

Then he smiled past the ache in his chest, pressed one soft kiss to her lips and gently set her back in her seat.

But not a single word would emerge from his crowded throat, so instead he turned the key in the ignition and headed back into town.

With Caroline staring at him.

CHAPTER ELEVEN

SHE WOULD ESCAPE at the first opportunity.

They'd reached town; it was four-thirty. Caroline's duty was finished. She'd done everything Elena had asked and more.

More than she could bear to remember. How could she have fallen apart like that? Humiliated herself once again in front of him? He hadn't given her so much as a look all the way back.

"What does she want?" Diego asked, staring through the windshield.

Caroline glanced ahead. Elena had stepped out in the street to catch his attention. "Diego, Mama Lalita called. She needs your help."

"What's wrong?" he demanded. "Is she hurt?"

Elena's curls bounced. "No, she's fine. She just said she had a little problem and you were the only one who could help." Her dark eyes glanced at Caroline, twinkling.

Caroline looked away. She didn't feel twinkly just now.

"I need to—" Diego sighed. "It can't wait?"

Elena shook her head. "She said it wouldn't take long, but she wanted me to catch you as soon as I could."

Good, Caroline thought. She could slip away to the cabin as soon as they arrived. Call Sam again or start walking to El Paso. She had to get out of here.

"All right," Diego conceded. To Caroline, he said, "I'll drop you off at the cabin first."

"I can walk from her house," she said.

Diego paused, looking at her.

She didn't return his gaze.

"Caroline—"

"Forget it. I shouldn't have—" She waved him off. "Just forget it, all right?"

"You don't understand—" he began.

"Stop it. Please. Just let me go—" *Home,* she almost said. But she couldn't go home. She wasn't even sure where that would be. "I really don't want to talk about it."

He cursed beneath his breath. "All right. For now," he warned. He turned the truck around and headed toward his grandmother's, and Caroline tried to be grateful.

Long before they reached Adelaida's, Diego began to frown and glance around at all the cars. "What the hell is this?"

In front of Adelaida's, a slender young woman with a swinging blond pageboy charged out of the gate, forcing Diego to hit the brakes.

"Oh, hell," he said. He shot Caroline a glare. "Did you know about this?"

Before she could answer, the young woman had raced to his side and opened the door. "Happy birthday, big brother!" She threw her arms around his neck. "We're throwing you a party. Are you surprised?"

"Of course I'm surprised." But affection blunted the grumble in his voice. "What have you done?" He turned off the key and slid out of the seat.

"It wasn't me—it was everyone." She grinned and hugged him again, then peered around his shoulder. "Hello."

Caroline nodded. "Hello."

"You must be the hotshot surgeon."

"Jenna—" Diego warned.

His sister slid past him and held out her hand. "I'm Jenna MacAllister, sister of Mr. Grumpy here. Welcome to La Paloma."

An awkward moment passed as Caroline extended her left hand.

"Oh—sorry. I forgot."

To hold anything against someone so wholesome and friendly was impossible. "No big deal," Caroline answered. "Pleased to meet you."

Jenna turned back to Diego. "Well, come on. Everyone's waiting."

"Jenna, I'm not a party person—you know that."

"Tell that to Mom," Jenna said.

Diego sighed. "Why aren't you in school?"

"You can't boss me around today," Jenna chided.

Suddenly Diego grinned, an easy smile Caroline had never seen. "I can boss you around any day, especially today." He looped one arm around her neck and pulled her close. "It's my birthday, remember?"

They both laughed, and the sound of it tore at Caroline's heart. She could barely remember the carefree laughter she once shared with her sisters.

Jenna wrapped one arm around his waist, but leaned past to speak to Caroline. "Come with us. The whole family wants to meet you."

"They're all here?" Diego asked. "Even—"

Jenna nodded. "Every one of them. Zane flew in on a private jet." She made a face. "Show-off. He picked up Cade in Utah and met Jesse in El Paso. Mom's in it up to her eyeballs. Dad tried to tell her you'd hate this, but the entire village wanted to do it, and it fell right in line with Mom's plans."

"You go on," Caroline urged. "I'll just run over to the cabin. I need to make a call, but I'll come by later."

Diego's eyes narrowed. He hesitated, but Jenna pulled him with her. "Just don't be too long," she warned. "Or my mother will be on your doorstep." Then they were off, Jenna chattering nonstop.

Caroline watched them go, Diego's step reluctant

but his affection obvious. She heard the mariachi music tuning up and listened to the cheerful, excited voices. He deserved this. It would do him good. Pull him out of hiding.

But for her...it was time to go. She slipped from the pickup and headed toward the cabin.

She tried Sam again, to no avail. She would make more calls to try to secure transportation, but first she wanted a shower.

She stood in it so long the hot water ran out as she tried to understand the jumble of feelings inside her. Part of her wanted to join the party, to watch the haunted Diego being toasted by those who loved him so. To spend a little more time among people who'd become dear to her.

But a wiser part told her that to do so would only make leaving harder. She dried herself off, studying the hand that felt stronger than before. She experimented with movement, eagerly noting that she could extend her fingers a little more without bracing her wrist. It always seemed to happen like this, little or no progress, then a sudden leap to a new stage just when she'd given up.

She stared into the bathroom mirror. Maybe it was almost over. Hope stirred, not the hope that came from pure stubborn refusal to consider anything else, but an honest optimism, a sense that maybe at last her nightmare was nearly done. That she really would get her life back.

For a minute, she wanted to run to the party and tell Diego. He would understand, better than anyone, just what this improvement meant.

The thought of leaving suddenly pierced her to the bone. Maybe he would come with her—

No. To urge that would be wrong. Cruel, both to him and everyone here.

They needed him. He was much loved.

So she would stay put tonight. It wasn't as though it was the first time she'd been on the outside looking in. Everything would be less complicated if she just made calls until she'd found a way to leave in the morning.

That settled, she opened the bathroom door and headed for her phone—

"Hello."

Caroline grabbed at her towel, staring at the woman in her living room. "Who are you? What do you want?"

Then she caught a good look at eyes she'd seen before, more gray than blue but unmistakably derived from this woman.

"You're Diego's mother." Everything else was hard to credit. This woman was small and slender, shorter than Caroline by two or three inches and just as blond. "You can't possibly be old enough," she blurted.

The woman laughed. "Oh, dear. Adelaida said I

would like you.'' She crossed the floor. ''I'm Grace MacAllister, and you're Dr. Malone.''

''Caroline, please.'' She clutched at the towel and looked down in dismay. ''Excuse me. I wasn't expecting—''

''You needn't bother on my account, but how about if I start us some tea while you change for the party?''

''I wasn't planning—''

Grace MacAllister waved her off. ''Of course you must attend. Perhaps you know Diego well enough to realize that parties are not his thing. He'd like to have you there. As a matter of fact, he was going to come after you himself, but I wasn't sure I'd be able to get him to come back if he ever escaped.'' She smiled.

Caroline had to smile in return. ''He wasn't too happy about my part in getting him there.''

''Well, then, you understand. Please come back with me. My son might forgive me sooner.'' She cocked her head and peered at Caroline. ''You're driving him crazy, you know. I can tell.''

''What?'' Caroline tensed. ''I'm not doing any such thing, Mrs. MacAllister, and anyway—''

''Grace. And I know it's none of my business except, you see, Diego is my firstborn. I learned about being a mother from him. I love each one of my children in a wholly special way, but there is something about your firstborn that—'' She waved one hand. "I can't quite explain it, but you'll understand one day."

Why did a pang hit her just then? "I doubt I will," she said stiffly. "My career doesn't leave much time for anything else."

"Oh, dear," his mother said. "There I go again. Of course you're right. Marriage and family aren't for everyone." Lightning-quick, she shifted topics. "You go ahead and get dressed, and we'll walk over together."

In an odd way, Diego's mother reminded Caroline of an aspect of Ivy she'd forgotten. Even as a girl, Ivy's sweetness had contained an edge of determination. Woe betide the person who stood between her and what she wanted for those she loved.

Grace MacAllister seemed much the same, if more practiced. Caroline had heard of steel magnolias before, but she wasn't sure she'd ever met one. Somehow she'd expected the expression to connote someone more brittle, but she realized her mistake now. Grace's will might be steel, but her polish provided the best camouflage Caroline had ever witnessed.

She would fight like a tiger for her son. Candor might be in order. "Diego's driving me crazy, too. It would be better for both of us if I just went my own way. I'm going to leave tomorrow."

Headed   for   the   kitchen,   Grace   turned.

"Funny...Adelaida didn't tell me you were a coward." Blue eyes challenged her.

It wasn't what Caroline expected. She'd thought Diego's mother would gladly help her pack to be rid of her. "I'm merely being logical. My life is elsewhere. Diego's is here. What's between us will fade with time."

Those eyes so like Diego's turned soft. "Oh, you poor dear. You've got it bad, don't you?" She crossed the floor. "Not that I blame you. Diego's father turned me inside out from the first moment. The only saving grace was that he was just as crazed over me."

"You don't understand. Diego and I aren't like that. There's nothing between us, really. We haven't even—" She could have bitten off her tongue.

His mother laughed gaily. "Oh my, no wonder he's so touchy. He's as hotblooded as his father. He must be miserable—"

"Mrs. MacAllister—" Caroline interrupted.

"Grace," she reminded her. "And I know you're right. That, especially, should be none of my business." This time her gaze was full of love and heartache. "But he's suffered so much and for so long. His heart isn't a warrior's heart. Oh, he was good at it—they expected him to rise as high as he wanted one day. But no matter how strong or capable Diego is, his heart has always been bigger still. Compassion runs deep in him, and what he experienced wounded him far worse than the terrible damage to his body. I was afraid he'd never get over losing his men, until I saw him today. I knew immediately that something had changed." She crossed to Caroline and took her hand. "I think you're responsible."

"I can't—" Caroline whispered. "I have to go back, and he has to stay." To her horror, her voice faltered.

The older woman touched her cheek. "Sometimes life doesn't give us answers that are easy to see, but they're there nonetheless. You just have to get quiet and move out of the way of the answer your heart needs."

Caroline just shook her head. "You don't understand." And a week's worth of hours wouldn't be long enough to explain. "It's not that I don't think Diego is—" Her voice fell away. "It just can't work, that's all. It will only hurt more if I go over there."

"It will hurt either way." Grace MacAllister relinquished her hand and stepped back, voice turning brisk. "But I don't think you are truly a coward, nor do I think you want to insult my son and his grandmother and a whole lot of people who want to honor them both. Am I right?"

Caroline let anger shore up the soft places that hurt too much. "People don't normally call me a coward," she said, voice chilling. "Nor would they get away with it if they did."

Grace's eyes sparkled, and she nodded. "Good. That's the woman I thought I was going to meet." She turned. "I'll have the tea ready by the time you're dressed."

Caroline watched her go, wondering if this small woman ran roughshod over her entire family like this.

Then, with a smile of sincere admiration, she headed for her bedroom and began to dress.

DIEGO KNEW it was foolish, but he kept looking out over the heads of those assembled, seeking Caroline. It was one advantage of being one of the tallest people there.

Just then, another tall form broke his field of vision. "Here," Jesse said, handing him a beer. "Take your mind off her with this."

Diego accepted the bottle. "Off who?"

"I wasn't born yesterday, you know." Jesse's eyes were dark with concern. It was as if they'd switched birth order when Diego was wounded, Jesse serving as fierce protector of his elder brother.

A hard clap on Diego's back almost had him spilling his beer. "So where's *la doctora?*" his brother Zane asked. "I want to see this woman who's got everyone talking."

Sometimes families were a real pain, Diego thought. He went for a casual shrug. "I don't know. I don't keep her calendar."

"Don't even keep it full?" Zane asked. Then his brows drew down. He peered at Diego more closely. "Uh-oh."

"Uh-oh what?" Diego snapped.

The man over whom millions of American women panted stepped back, lifted his hands, palms out, grinning. "So it's like that, is it?"

Diego scanned the faces of his brothers—Cade, too, had just arrived at his side—and cursed beneath his breath.

"Leave him alone, guys," Jesse ordered.

Diego could see his younger brothers mentally cataloguing information, trying to calculate the next move. Then Cade's eyes widened as he stared past Diego's shoulder.

"Well..." he commented. "I see the attraction."

Diego turned toward Mama Lalita's gate.

His mother at her side, Caroline stood there, seemingly as though she'd rather be anywhere else. Resembling no Caroline he'd ever seen before.

Her dress was obviously from the city, expensive and classy. Simple in line and the palest jade, it floated down from her shoulders, skimming her slender frame, kissing her curves until it stopped just at her ankles. On her feet were sandals strapped with slim bands of leather, each topped with a sprinkle of tiny flowers. Around her neck she wore a delicate locket and from her ears swung thin loops of gold.

Elegant, she looked to him. And frightened.

Before he could consider the wisdom of it, he shoved his beer into Jesse's hand and headed toward her.

He spared his mother a glance. Her eyes warned him to take it easy. He acknowledged her with a nod. "Thanks, Mom." He leaned forward and kissed his mother's cheek.

Grace's hand lingered on his jaw for just a second as she brought her mouth to his ear. "I almost didn't get her here."

He touched the hand of the woman who'd filled his life with love and smiled. Then he turned to Caroline. "I'm glad you came," he said simply.

Her gaze locked on his. "So you forgive me for distracting you all day?"

"Knowing my mother, I doubt you had much choice." He narrowed his eyes at his mother. "Is there nothing you won't stoop to?"

His mother held out her hands. "I didn't—"

Diego was already shaking his head.

"Well, all right, I was involved, but I didn't start it." She pressed her hand to his cheek again. "They love you, son. All of us do." In her eyes, a sorrow bloomed. "But, Diego, don't let anyone force you into stay—"

"Mama," he shushed her. "It's all right. I'm doing what I want."

Mostly.

Then he noticed Caroline trying to slip away and grabbed her wrist. "Don't go," he urged. "Please."

Her eyes told him she felt frightened and trapped. He almost released her, until he heard the sounds of his family at his back. "Stay with me," he murmured. "I'm your only hope."

He grinned, but she didn't relax. Still, he drew her closer.

A big hand clapped his shoulder. "Happy birthday, son," boomed Hal MacAllister.

Diego turned toward the man who'd always treated him as his own. "Thank you." He hugged Hal, exchanging slaps on the back. "May I present Dr. Caroline Malone?"

"Thought you'd never get around to it," Hal said, then moved his attention to Caroline. "So…Mercy Hospital, is it? Don't suppose that scalawag Sam Calvert is still running things."

"He is," Caroline answered. "And he's still a scalawag."

Hal's laughter thundered, and Diego felt Caroline relaxing. Soon they were comparing notes on common acquaintances, and Caroline's green eyes grew animated.

"Move over, Dad," Zane complained. "Don't hog the girl. You've already got yours."

Diego bit back a laugh as Caroline's face became the slightest bit starstruck.

"I do at that," Hal chuckled. "But I hear you're

about to marry that femme fatale from your last film.''

"You've got to stop reading the tabloids, Dad.'' Zane rolled his eyes and took Caroline's good hand. "Don't listen to him. Let me take you away from all this, Doc.'' He waggled his brows. "I have my own plane.''

The ever-so-serious Dr. Malone didn't seem to know how to respond. Diego didn't think flirting had been much in her repertoire.

Cade stepped in next. "Forget the pretty boy. I'm headed to Alaska on a shoot. You look like a woman who actually knows how to read scientific magazines. Zane here still reads comic books.''

Zane punched Cade lightly. "This woman has too much class to live in hiking boots and sleep on the ground. Buzz off.''

Diego saw Caroline glance beside him, where his silent, overprotective brother stood. "Get lost, children,'' he said to Zane and Cade. "Caroline, this is my brother Jesse.''

Jesse nodded, never much of one for smiling. "Pleased to meet you.''

His restraint seemed to calm her. "Thank you.'' She hesitated, scanning them all. He'd never seen her look this shy.

Physical proximity was the last thing either of them should dare right now, but he couldn't just leave her at the mercy of his boisterous family.

"Want to dance?" he asked, then held his breath, waiting for her to refuse.

She glanced around.

"I learned to tango for my last film," Zane offered. "Diego can't dance worth a damn."

"I'm sure Diego dances just fine." She tilted her chin.

Zane dropped the affectionate ribbing and nodded. "You're right," he said with quiet force. "Diego does everything well."

At last, Caroline smiled freely at Zane. Then she turned that smile on Diego, but it began to fade as though she, too, recognized the folly of any more involvement.

It wasn't a discussion they could have here, so he simply drew her into the crowd and took her into his arms.

"Zane's right," he said. "I could dance once, but I'm not graceful anymore."

She frowned. "Zane shouldn't—"

"No—" he interrupted. "He's doing exactly what I asked. I got so damn sick of them all tiptoeing around me I told them I'd kick all their behinds if they didn't start acting normally." Seeing her confusion, he continued. "You never had brothers, so you wouldn't know. It's all about pecking order, about challenging the one above you." When she still looked mystified, he tried again. "We used to wrestle one another down, trash-talk at every opportunity—'' He shrugged. "Just…brothers who love one another.''

"Love? That's how you show it?"

Diego smiled at her incredulity. "Yeah. Then I got hurt, and everyone tiptoed around me as though I was crystal that would shatter.''

"They were worried.''

"Of course they were. But the more they danced around, the more I had to wonder if I was kidding myself that I'd ever get back on my feet, if there was something they all knew but weren't telling me.''

She shook her head. "I—I don't get it. If they insult you, it makes you feel better?''

Diego laughed. "Yeah. Something like that.'' He drew her close. "Is it okay for me to hold your hand like this?'' He indicated her injured hand.

Puzzlement gave way to excitement. "I think it's getting better. Today I didn't need my wrist brace to have the strength to punch the cash register buttons, and I actually released a couple of cans without help.''

"I noticed you using it more with patients as the day wore on.'' He didn't let himself think about how it meant she would leave sooner. "Congratulations.''

The wonder in her eyes was something he'd have liked to generate. "Thank you. It felt terrific to see patients again.''

He smiled. "You're good with them."

"I've never had much chance to interact on that level." She grinned. "My patients are unconscious for much of the time we're together."

Diego chuckled. "Don't give you a lot of flack that way, though."

Appreciation flickered in her gaze, and he had to try harder not to pay attention to how good she felt in his arms.

"That's true, but it's such a great feeling to work with people to solve their health problems. To be part of—" She broke off. The frown skipped over her face again, and she lifted her gaze to his. "I'm thinking I can go back sooner."

"Your month isn't up. What will your occupational therapist say?"

Her jaw stiffened. "When he sees that the hand is better, he'll change his mind."

Part of Diego wanted to clap a hand over her mouth, to tell her that he didn't want to hear any more. He stared out across the crowd until he could master the turmoil inside. He tried for a casual shrug. "We knew you would go."

"It's been...wonderful here," she said. "People have been so kind." She lifted her eyes to his. "You've been—" She stopped and swallowed. "I'm not sure how to explain, Diego. I never planned to get involved." Her earnest gaze searched his. "But you were right. I'm a healer. I enjoyed house calls with you today. It's just that it made me more aware of all those back there whom I could help. People depending on me to make them well. Needing skills I have that I can't use here.''

He wanted to protest that she could use her skills anywhere. That she had other skills besides surgery.

That he needed her—

No. That was going too far. Opening himself up to that was the height of folly.

''I understand,'' he said, biting back all the other words.

''Do you?'' Worried green eyes studied his.

His chest crowded with something hot and painful; his throat filled with words he dared not say. His mind balked at revealing any of it to a woman for whom he'd be only a memory soon.

''Of course,'' he managed. Then anger steadied him. ''I know what it's like to have other people depending on you, Caroline.''

She looked grateful, even if doubt still hovered. ''Thank you.'' She opened her mouth as if to say more, then shook her head.

Just as well. Words would do nothing to heal what burned inside him. But just to be perverse, he drew her closer. When she came without protest, he wanted to shake his fist at the heavens. *Damn you for bringing her to me when you knew she wouldn't stay.*

But Diego had learned some harsh lessons about

what you could change and what you had to let go. He wasn't ready to relinquish her yet, though, so he simply rested his cheek on the top of her hair and tried to still his mind as though he were immersed in the healing waters of his spring.

And when her other hand crept up to cradle the back of his neck, he bit back the urge to howl at a moon shining down on them as if this were an ordinary night. As if they were any man and woman beginning the first steps of a dance that could end in what so many took for granted: the chance for a shared future.

RAMÓN DREW DIEGO UP in front of the band while Caroline melted back toward the edge of the crowd. She watched the people hugging Diego, clasping his shoulder, shaking his hand. Watched their eyes light with the hope that he'd given them.

"Permiso," Ramón called. *"Atención, por favor."*

The noisy crowd began to quiet.

A hand touched her shoulder. The warmth of it brought a soul-deep sigh from inside Caroline. A piercing longing for its comfort.

"You are troubled, child," Adelaida said.

Caroline dropped her chin to her chest and swallowed hard.

The warm hand stroked down her spine, and Caroline wanted to weep.

"You are leaving."

Caroline's head whipped around to face eyes dark with sympathy. "It's not because—you've been so good to me—everyone has." She reached for the old woman's hand. "But especially you...I never had a grandmother. I used to wish—" The past wasn't what mattered now. "If I could place an order, I'd want a grandmother exactly like you."

Mama Lalita's other hand cupped her cheek. "My heart is not reserved only for those of my blood. Leave us if you must, but come back, *m'ija,* when you need the love we offer you."

Caroline bit her lip. She folded the old woman into her arms and searched for words that could never come near expressing what this woman meant to her. "I'm so sorry," she whispered. "So very sorry—I have to go—"

Caroline tore herself from Adelaida's arms and plunged through the wall of bodies at her back. Vaguely she heard Ramón begin to speak of Diego, heard the crowd roar out its affection for a man who deserved all of that and more.

A strong hand halted her.

"How can you do this to him?" Jesse's dark eyes snapped. He'd obviously heard her say she was leaving. His voice was deceptively calm. "Not good enough for you, Doctor?"

She recoiled in shock. "How could you think—

Diego's the best man I ever met." She blinked back tears. "Please—don't make a scene. Just let me go."

His anger hummed like a taut bowstring.

Jesse probed her gaze, and she saw in his eyes that she'd come up wanting. "Go ahead—run. Get the hell away from my brother. He deserves better."

She forced herself not to flinch. "Move out of my way and I will."

Jesse stepped aside but didn't look away.

Caroline took one step past him, then halted. "You're right, you know." Her voice caught, and she barely managed to continue. "He deserves much better than me."

Behind her the crowd cheered, chanting Diego's name.

And Caroline ran.

CHAPTER TWELVE

A JUBILANT SAM HAD promised that a car would be there by ten in the morning to pick her up. A hospital board member had put his plane at their disposal; she'd be home by early afternoon. Don Henderson would clear his schedule to see her that same day, and they'd outline the new game plan for her rehabilitation.

She might be back in the surgical suite by the end of the year. Back where she belonged, she told herself firmly. Back in the life she'd fought so hard to make.

She should be thrilled.

She was. Really.

Down the road, the mariachi music had stopped. The cars were gone, the sound of their engines dying away.

All Caroline could hear now was the ever-present wind.

And the sick thud of her heart.

She sank to the bed, where her suitcases lay open, too full now with her share of Elena's *tesoros*.

clean, sharp arrow through the water. Caroline tried to make herself turn away. She couldn't.

Then Diego emerged. At his right hip and down his leg she saw the web of scarring, and her practiced eye told her that he'd endured far more agony than he'd ever admitted.

Caroline hugged the shadows. Every other man she'd known in her life paled beside him. So many contrasts...so much mystery...such undeserved pain.

He sank to the ground again, his back to her. The spring gurgled in the crisp night air. The moon silvered highlights over the blue-black shadows of his hair. Droplets of water clung to the valley between the muscles ridging his back.

Caroline shivered.

He was still, so very still. Spine straight and head high, he sat cross-legged, hands resting on his knees, palms up. A shudder rippled through him, then his chest expanded in the long, slow breaths of meditation.

He began to chant, and the sound of his voice reached deep inside her.

The fine hairs rose on her body. She took a step toward him, then paused, unbearably drawn to him but so unsure what to do.

Diego's head lifted. She heard the quick intake of his breath.

She made ready to escape.

"No." His voice enveloped her, dusky and somber. "Don't go." He rose and faced her.

"Lobo came after me. I thought you were hurt."

He glanced away. "No. Only…tired."

He was so alone. Such a beautiful man—damaged, yes, but more powerful for his suffering. He could have been a warlock, an ancient sorcerer, a shaman. Something beyond his physical being spilled into the air around him, something that almost frightened her, though she knew to her bones he would never cause her harm.

"You're troubled, *querida.*"

"I—" Her chest felt tight. "Diego, there's a car coming to pick me up in the morning."

"You already said you would go. I won't try to talk you out of it," he said, still extending the hand, his seer's eyes so compassionate. So compelling. "But you need peace as much as I do. This last night, let me share my spring with you."

Around and between them a web of yearning spun, silken strands so entwined that to cut them would have required a swift, sharp blade. Even if she'd possessed the strength, she could never have summoned the will.

Not tonight.

This last night, he'd said. He wouldn't try to stop her from leaving after all. A part of her eased, even as another part mourned that the decision wouldn't be taken from her hands.

"If I didn't have patients waiting—"

"But you do," he said. "Our paths part here, it seems. If we cannot change that, let us give ourselves the gift of one night to be simply Diego and Caroline."

She wanted that more than he'd ever know, but she sensed the pain waiting for dawn's light, an agony so huge she quailed from it already.

As if he could read her thoughts, Diego proffered a smile that was both bittersweet and chiding. "We are both strong, Caroline. We know how to survive what we must."

Yes. Something in his voice slid past the fear of the grief that lay on the horizon, made her reach for what shimmered before her, bright in its promise, if fleeting.

Caroline shoved past fear and bridged the distance between them in an act of faith beyond anything she'd ever dared.

Diego clasped her hand in his, and her eyes closed as she breathed in the scent and feel of him until she could barely fight back a clawing urge to devour him whole.

But though she felt desire flare through him in one long shudder, Diego didn't grab her and offer her the easy out of mindless need.

Instead, he gave her tenderness.

He led her to the water's edge and began to remove her clothes with a touch that would have seemed efficient and neutral if she hadn't felt his fingers tremble.

Out of character, Caroline stood before him passive and open, quivering with her own daring. Trusting him as she had trusted no one else in her life, she fastened her gaze on his face as though he held the key to questions she'd never dared to ask.

With careful movements, he slid her garments from her body until she was as naked as he. When she should have felt exposed, Caroline realized she felt strong.

And beautiful in his eyes.

She expected him to take her then, to ply her body with those hands that never ceased to make her long for their touch. To take her to the ground and feed on her as she wanted to feed on him.

Instead he picked her up and walked into the water.

The first shock stole her breath.

"Relax, *mi corazón*," he said. "Lie back."

Oddly enough, she found that she could. The heat pouring off his body countered the water's chill. Diego kept his arms beneath her as he laid her on the surface and urged her to float. "Let the waters cleanse away the past," he said. "Accept the healing they offer."

How she wanted that. Water slid through her hair like cool fingers. Over the front of her, Diego's warmth shielded her from the night's breeze. Peace mingled with a desire so piercing she wanted to groan against the delicious bite of it.

His hands slid away, and she tensed.

"Sh-h," he soothed. "You're safe…let go."

She obeyed. Somehow even without touching her, he made her feel secure. Cradled in the soft water, surrounded by his care. She couldn't relinquish the wanting of him, no. What woman could, faced with a man like Diego?

But the wanting gave spice to the refuge if she stopped fighting the pull of him and let herself revel. Luxuriate in both the peace and the promise that the night would hold more.

Perhaps more than either of them could bear.

"Sh-h." A smile danced over his lips. "You're thinking again."

Caroline smiled back, feeling strong and free. Exhilarated by the piquancy of being both cherished and craved. Emboldened by the knowledge that they had only this night to build memories that must last for years.

So she did something totally unlike her.

She teased. Spread her arms over her head and displayed her body as artlessly as a child.

Or perhaps a seductress, secure that he would keep her safe. That she could poke a stick into the panther's cage. Dance on the edge of his control and see if she could break it.

She discovered she could.

With a muttered oath, Diego yanked her up against his hard body.

And, let the beast free.

Caroline's own control snapped then. She wrapped her legs around his waist and gripped his hair in one hand, giving as good as she got.

They joined battle, two powerful spirits locked in mortal combat. Two hearts fighting odds they could not beat, furious with fates they could not change. Two bodies filled with rage and desire, seeking completion that went beyond the physical, past all common sense.

Suddenly, Diego strode from the water and laid her down on the grass, surging inside her before she could catch her breath.

Caroline made a sound low in her throat and clawed closer still.

Fierce and fast and furious, each tried to make up for all they'd wanted from the first day, all they could not resolve in any other way. They fought like warrior angels past all the barriers the world had cast between them—

Into a place of dreams. Of stunning, terrifying bliss. A place where hearts met, souls mingled, forever changed.

As they fell to earth, Diego reversed their positions, wrapping his arms so tightly around the woman splayed over him that she could barely breathe.

For a moment, they lay there, gasping, past all speech. Caroline was still searching for firm footing, scrambling back to familiar ground—

When Diego began to touch her again, this time with a tenderness she could not fight. Could not fathom. Could only lie there and soak in like rain on the desert of her soul.

After he'd led her up winding, verdant paths to a sweetness that brought tears streaming from her eyes, Caroline soaked in a bliss she knew she would never feel again. Would long for all of her life.

Weeping, she held him close, gripping so hard she could feel his heart thud against hers.

Then, with a grief that scored like acid, she sought the strength to slip away.

Diego tightened his grasp. To hell with his vow. "Don't run this time," he whispered, the beat of his heart still racing. "Stay, *querida*. There's a home for you here."

She turned her face into his shoulder, and he felt her fingers curl into his sides. Felt her tremble.

She attempted to speak, then swallowed hard. Tried again.

Diego wanted to press his hand to her mouth to stop words he knew he didn't want to hear.

Instead he forced himself to lie still.

"I can't." In her voice he heard grating regret, a gift he would treasure in the dark days to come. "Just as these people need you, there are others who need me." She tilted her head to look at him. "I do have something to contribute, Diego. It's not all just ambition."

"I know. But your contribution is greater than you think. It isn't limited to the scalpel." He caressed her cheek. "You're a healer, Caroline, whatever method you must use. Within the driven woman is someone who cares deeply."

Gratitude softened her eyes. Sorrow darkened them. "Thank you. I wish—" Her lashes slid lower, and he saw tears shimmer. "I left patients back there who are depending on me. My hand is getting stronger. I have to go back and care for them."

She looked at him then, and through the tears he saw the longing. "I wish you could come with me. The sky would be the limit for you. I'd do anything I could to help."

How a part of him wanted that still. How he had to work to banish it. "It's not my path, *querida.* These are my people now."

Slender fingers rose to stroke his jaw. He thought of how she'd guarded that hand so carefully and was moved by the trust that she would use it so freely on him.

"I'm sorry," she said. "I'm making it worse." One finger traced over his eyelid, and the tenderness of it undid him. "I admire you so much," she whispered. "You are the most honorable man I've ever met."

His gaze was ravaged. "I've killed, Caroline. I've let others down—"

She halted his words with her hand. "Don't. None of that matters." With one fist she touched her heart. "I know who you are. In here I know."

Diego clasped her fist and opened it. Eyes closed, he kissed her palm, unable to speak past the ache and longing, the rage at life and fate and duties he hadn't asked for.

"Oh, Diego...I—"

He stopped her with a kiss, then a caress—

One more time, they tasted. Surrendered. Cherished. Slid into a healing sleep.

Caroline awoke as dawn beckoned, watching Diego with eyes that burned. With a heavy heart, she attempted a sign of the cross over him as she'd seen Adelaida do, lingering with her hand outstretched above his heart.

Then she dressed quickly and slipped away, forbidding herself to look back.

Never knowing what it cost Diego to lie so still—

And watch her walk out of his life.

CHAPTER THIRTEEN

THE EQUIPMENT HAD ARRIVED right on schedule, as Caroline had promised. Diego had worked day and night to be ready for it. Mama Lalita had swept the clinic clean with incense, herbs and prayers; the priest had added the church's blessings.

Now Diego saw patients all day, went home at night knowing he'd done what he could. That he'd earned his rest.

But sleep proved elusive. For almost a month, his nights had been a state of war. He had the pottery to show for it as he sought refuge in clay. He'd never produced better work.

And never cared about it less.

Funny that although Caroline had been both rude and cynical in the beginning, he missed that sharp edge most. She challenged him. Made him think. Made him uncomfortable, yes, but he'd never felt more alive than when she'd been standing toe-to-toe with him, those green eyes daring him to convince her.

He couldn't let himself reflect on her sweetness,

on the vulnerability that worried him so. How did she fare, back in the jungle? How was her hand? Did anyone care?

Of course they did. She was Mercy's rainmaker, Mercy's star.

But did anyone understand that beneath that warrior angel's face lurked a heart that needed a tender touch? That she could be hurt?

Lobo whined beside him. Diego dug his fingers in the dog's ruff and held on. "She's where she wants to be, boy. We have to leave her alone."

But everywhere he looked, Caroline had marked his world. He didn't visit his spring anymore; the peace had fled. All he could see there was her, slender as a taper, smooth as marble.

Burning with a fire that had scorched them both.

TEACHING ROUNDS WERE the next step on Caroline's comeback. "So how would you approach this case?" she asked a bright-eyed intern who reminded her all too much of herself.

The young woman didn't blink, rattling off a list of tests she'd conduct and what the results would tell her.

The suggestions were dead-on. Caroline couldn't have done better, but she found that she couldn't settle for simple procedures now. "How is he feeling?"

The young woman ticked off his symptoms, a slight frown between her eyes.

"No—" Caroline interrupted. "I don't mean physically. What is he thinking now? Is he scared? What will he assume if you're ordering all these tests? Will it increase his worry? How do you propose to incorporate his family into the picture?"

All six interns regarded her with owlish eyes. "What does his family have to do with it?" one brave soul asked.

A question she herself would have asked once. "We cannot treat only the symptoms," she said. "We have to deal with the whole patient. That means his mind and spirit, as well as his heart."

"But we're doing surgery," one protested.

Caroline listened to her own words with rue. *Diego would love seeing me in this position.* "Our concern for the patient can't begin and end in the O.R.," she said. "Nor can it be limited to the span of an office visit." A warmth crept over her as she felt, for the first time in months, a sureness she'd thought never to know again. In her mind's eye, she could see Adelaida's serene face. Feel the old woman's peace steal into her heart.

"Western medicine has accomplished miracles, many of them in your lifetimes." She scanned the faces, so young, so ambitious. "But we are healers," she said. "And the tradition goes back for centuries before the scalpel, before antibiotics, before technology separated our minds from our bodies, our souls from our skin—"

Caroline broke off, realizing that only one of the six was really listening. Cast back into the days of her internship, she remembered the pervading sense of exhaustion, of wondering if she'd make it through that next double shift. The energy to argue philosophical viewpoints was beyond them at this moment.

"Tell you what," she said. "Anyone who's off tonight, meet me at Maguire's at eight. I'll buy you a beer, and we'll argue about this. That's all for now."

Earnest faces sagged in relief. "Thanks, Dr. Malone. See you at eight," said the girl with all the answers—who might actually come but likely wouldn't listen. Holistic medicine did not make the big bucks, and this girl's ambition crackled around her like chain lightning.

The group dispersed, and Caroline turned to head back to her office to review some charts before time for therapy.

"A little missionary work, Queenie?" Judd Carter stood only a few feet away, no doubt having heard the whole thing. "Not your usual style."

She looked at the man who'd once been able to engender such ire in her. An image of Diego rose in her mind, and she could only feel sorry for the man before her, so sure of his superiority but so much less of a man. "What do you want, Judd?" She braced herself for more ridicule.

But he only studied her, frowning slightly. "What happened to you out there, Caroline?"

"Out where?" The last person in the world with whom she'd discuss Diego Montalvo or the valley would be this man who would never understand.

"You've lost your edge," he mused. "Be careful or even if you get the hand back, it won't matter."

Caroline cast a glance at the hand that could now hold a pen, that could deal with buttons and do needlework but was not yet ready to operate. A frisson of fear shimmered down her spine. She had to get the hand back. She would do whatever it took.

Her chin tilted, and she met Judd's eyes with her own unyielding stare. "So sweet of you to worry about me, Judd." She patted one cheek, wishing it were a slap. "I'm a lucky girl to have such great friends."

She slid past him, shoving down on the cold, jellied fear that he was right.

Something inside her had been changed forever, it seemed. There was therapy for her hand, but she had no idea what to do with the heart that had once been easily guarded, once so bulletproof. The old Caroline Malone had been revered for being hard and unshakable, skilled and single-minded.

That Caroline had been shattered by her time in the valley like the brittle glass she'd once been.

Elena, Mariela, Ramón, Adelaida…none of them cared that she was the best, that she could climb to the top of the mountain. They'd seen her damaged and hadn't blinked.

They'd liked her for herself, battered and brittle. They'd accepted the woman no one here knew.

While she couldn't seem to find the woman she'd been.

She was a fraud, but no one here understood it yet. She couldn't go back and didn't know how to go forward.

But Judd Carter already suspected. Soon others would, too.

And she'd left behind the only person who would truly understand what it was to belong nowhere. To face inventing oneself again.

She'd abandoned that man beside a spring. Turned up her nose at what he'd offered, certain she belonged here, that resuming her life was all that was important.

Her patients *were* important. Not being able to operate yet was maddening, but at least she could see them, could follow their care. But she found herself wondering about Trini Vargas, thinking about Mariela's child. Hoping Adelaida was taking things easier; wishing she knew if Diego's clinic was operating.

A part of her had stayed in La Paloma, and every

day—every patient—brought a fresh reminder of her loss.

She didn't fit in yet. Surely in time she would, but right now, no matter how she filled the days, the nights were endless.

The only bright spot on the horizon was the news she'd gotten yesterday from the private investigator.

He'd found Ivy. Near, so near. Less than two hours away.

Her first impulse had been to race out the door and drive to Palo Verde.

But fear had stopped her. She couldn't bear it if Ivy didn't want to see her. Her time in La Paloma had opened her eyes to a different way. For so many years, she'd clung to thoughts of the future, unable to bear remembering her past.

But she'd seen the love of family, how it made poverty unimportant, how it bestowed strength. Diego and Adelaida, Diego and his brothers, his mother's fierce devotion, his little sister's adoration.

For the first time, Caroline realized that she was lonely.

That she'd been lonely for most of her life.

Now she was regretting asking the investigator to contact Ivy first. She wasn't usually a coward; it was just that this was so important—

"Dr. Malone?"

Caroline jerked out of her musings. The unit secretary stood before her. "Yes?"

"Mr. Calvert has been paging you."

"He has?" The intercom system had once been hardwired into her brain. "I didn't hear it." And wondered how that could be.

The young woman nodded. "He sent me to track you down. He'd like you to come to his office as soon as possible."

"Did he say why?"

"No."

Caroline frowned. She had no idea what Sam could want with her. "All right. Tell him I'll be there as soon as I finish the charts."

"He—" The young woman seemed unsure of herself. "He said it was urgent."

Caroline shrugged. "Okay. I'll head there now."

All the way up in the elevator, she cast about in her mind, trying to figure out what could be so crucial. She found her way to Sam's office and prepared to knock.

Instead of his usual invitation to enter, Sam surprised her by slipping through the door and holding it closed behind him. His brow filled with lines of concern.

"What's up, Sam?"

He grasped her elbow and escorted her across the hall. "I have no idea how to handle this," he said, running fingers through his hair.

"What? Tell me what's going on," she demanded. Then her heart stalled. "Has Don said something to you about my hand?"

"No, it's not that—" He shook his head, still frowning. Then he pinned her with his gaze. "Tell me about your family, Caroline."

"What?" She was still trying to process the abrupt switch of topics. "What does that have to do with my hand?"

"Caroline, it's not about your hand. It's about—"

Just then, his office door opened, and a woman stepped out, small and blond and curvy. In her arms was a baby girl with a shock of dark hair. Behind her stood a tall man with hawk-sharp features, his hands settled protectively on the woman's shoulders.

The woman looked at her out of vivid blue eyes that almost looked like—

Caroline's heart thudded once, hard. "Ivy?" She glanced at Sam, then back. "Is it really you?"

"Caroline—" The woman's smile was as bright as the sun despite the tears rolling down her cheeks. "Oh, Caroline, I couldn't wait another minute after the investigator contacted us. We've been searching for you—"

The tall man eased the child from Ivy's arms. Ivy closed the distance between them, folding her taller sister into her embrace.

For a second, Caroline froze. She'd never been touched much, except at La Paloma—

But Ivy was a toucher, always had been.

Caroline reared back, breathless. "I can't believe—wait, you were searching for me? But I was—he just found you—"

Ivy grabbed her again, crying and laughing and hugging her hard. It felt good. It felt wonderful. Oh, God, she was going to cry—

Caroline sagged into Ivy's embrace. She was barely aware that somehow they'd moved into Sam's office, that the tall man and Sam had vanished. That she was seated on a love seat with the sister she hadn't seen in twenty years.

That mingled in with the confusion and gratitude and wonder was the thought that Diego had been right. That she'd needed her sisters for a very long time.

She sat up straight, wiping her cheeks with the palms of her hands. Ivy produced a wad of tissues from a hidden pocket and finished the job, then gave her more tissues to blow her nose.

"You haven't really changed, have you?" Caroline said. "Still the little mother."

Odd currents shifted through Ivy's blue eyes: joy and pride shot through with darker currents of sorrow. "But you—" Ivy said. "You're a doctor? A surgeon?" She shook her head. "You were always the smartest person I ever knew, but how on earth did you get from runaway to this—" Ivy's hands spread to note the surroundings. "Mr. Calvert praised you to the skies—that is, when he wasn't worrying over how you'd take the news.''

"Me? I was afraid that—'' She struggled to catch her breath. "I didn't know if you'd want to see me. Ivy, I should have looked for you before, and I should have been braver about contacting you myself, but—'' She grabbed Ivy's hand. "Where's Chloe? Have you found her?''

Ivy's eyes darkened. "No. Not yet—but Linc will manage it. There's nothing he can't do when he sets his mind to it.''

With a jolt, Caroline realized Ivy must be talking about the tall man. "Is he—are you married, Ivy? Is that your baby?''

Ivy leaped up. "Oh—Linc will be worried. He thought we should wait for you, but I just couldn't.''

Caroline chuckled. "You still lead with your heart, don't you?''

Ivy's blue eyes sparkled with laughter. "Some things never change. Come on, let's go find Linc—'' She grasped Caroline's hands to pull her up.

Caroline jerked her right hand away.

"I'm sorry. He told us, but I forgot—'' Ivy's cheeks burned scarlet.

"No, it's me who's sorry. It's better, really. I'm just in the habit of protecting it.''

Ivy went still. "There's so much I need to know about you.'' Her eyes filled again. "I was afraid I'd never see you again, and I've missed you so much.

I tried and tried to find you, but I never had enough money to do it right—'' Her voice broke.

Shame swept over Caroline. She'd had plenty of money for the past several years. ''I only tried once,'' she admitted. ''I should have done more. I was—'' She looked away. ''I told myself that I was better off alone.'' She met her sister's gaze, expecting condemnation.

Instead, she saw tenderness. And understanding. ''Daddy's leaving hurt us all,'' Ivy said. ''And Mother never really got over it.'' Her eyes were so sad now. ''I should have found a way to convince the social workers—''

''Stop.'' Caroline clasped her sister's hands, grateful she could grip again with both of them. ''I gave up too easily. I was the eldest. I should have stayed and fought instead of running away.''

Don't run, querida. *Why must you run?* Diego had seen the truth of her.

Ivy pulled her close again, hugging her hard. ''We were too young, just as they said. They would never have let us keep Chloe—'' Her voice turned fierce. ''But we're going to find her now.'' Ivy drew back. ''We're going to get her back. Linc will help us.'' Then Ivy's eyes widened. ''Is there someone in your life?''

Diego rose in her mind's eye, big and bold and strong.

Caroline shook her head. ''No. No one.''

Ivy's gaze narrowed. She'd always seen too much. "I want to hear about him when you're ready." She stroked Caroline's cheek. "But right now, I want you to meet the new members of your family."

Caroline followed as Ivy drew her from the room, refusing to let her hand go, trying to absorb the idea that this morning she'd been all but an orphan and now she had a sister, a big, handsome brother-in-law and a niece. And soon they would find Chloe.

It was all more than she could take in just yet. She wanted to cry and laugh—

And run and hide until she figured out how she felt about all of it. It made her think of the paradox of Diego, surrounded by love and yet so alone.

Ah, Diego, we're a pair, aren't we?

Even as the thought formed, she realized that maybe she did want to tell Ivy about Diego after all.

Then a sweet-smelling bundle was thrust into her arms.

"Oh." She looked down into a tiny face staring up at her with wide blue eyes. "Oh, aren't you a beauty?" She glanced over at Ivy, nestled into her husband's embrace.

"Her name is Amelia Caroline." Proud gray eyes met hers in a face as arresting in its own way as Diego's. "And I'm Linc Galloway, another of your sister's projects."

Caroline burst out laughing. Something about this

man spoke of a reserve equal to her own, yet Ivy's impact was clear in the teasing glint of his eyes, the tender smile, the obvious love binding the three of them into one unit.

How she envied them. Ivy had always had love to spare.

Then it hit her. "Caroline?" She glanced down at the baby, then up at Ivy, whose eyes glistened still.

"Amelia was Linc's mother's name. I would have given her Mother's name, too, but I wanted her to be strong like you," she added.

Caroline felt shame then. "You're the strong one, Ivy. It takes courage to keep your heart open."

"She told me I'd like you," Linc said, one hand stroking Ivy's shoulder. "That we had a lot in common." His gaze fixed on hers. "I left when I was eighteen and never went back," he said. "It took your sister to convince me that needing others wasn't a weakness."

This man had known hard times and heartache, she could see. She wasn't comfortable with his insights into her, but nothing in her life had been comfortable for months now, and she was beginning to wonder if she'd ever find that safe ground again.

Then a tiny hand fastened around her finger, and Caroline's heart melted. Amelia's eyes locked on hers, the rosebud mouth opening in a wide, gummy grin.

Her blood. This child shared her blood.

"Tesoro," she murmured, and suddenly Diego was with her, his beautiful, strong hands cradling another child.

"What?" Ivy asked.

Caroline blinked back tears. "Treasure," she answered. "She's a treasure." Then Caroline looked at her sister again. "Oh, Ivy, I've missed you," she whispered.

For the first time since she'd left a cool mountain spring and a sleeping hero, Caroline felt some of the ragged edges of her heart start to mend.

When Ivy embraced her this time, Caroline held nothing back.

Diego sat on his front porch, seeing none of the vista spread before him, cup of coffee going cold in his hand. Beside his chair, Lobo sat patiently, wolf eyes never leaving him.

Diego let his head fall against the high back of the rocking chair. The day had been long, like every day before it since—

No. Not tonight. I'm not thinking of her tonight.

He needed sleep, that was all. News of the clinic had spread fast; people were coming from farther away now, seeking the help they couldn't afford before. Elena and Mariela pitched in when they could; there was so much to be done, even with something as simple as he'd envisioned—records to be kept, supplies to be ordered, cleaning and sterilizing. It was rapidly growing into more than he could handle alone.

And then there was Trini. Diego had found a cardiologist at the base hospital, but the man spared little sympathy when he was overworked himself. It would be weeks before he could see Trini—if Diego could ever convince the old man to go all the way to El Paso.

Trini wanted Caroline.

He wasn't alone in that. In her short time, she'd left an indelible impression on many people.

Take himself.

In a lifetime of encounters with the opposite sex, Diego had enjoyed many women, had tried to leave each one with grace, making sure that she would have fond memories of their time together.

He'd never been the one left before. As much as that might once have hurt his pride, ego had little to do with his feelings now. He'd known from the beginning that she was temporary. Hell, he hadn't even liked her at first—prickly as a cactus, high-strung as any filly he'd ever had to tame.

But he knew more now of what made her that way.

He wanted to stand between her and the world. Wrap his love around her until it became the shield she needed to feel safe. He didn't think she'd ever had that.

He'd had it from birth. The battles he'd fought, the sense of not fitting in, had come from the wider world and from within himself, but never, not once, had anyone in his family made him feel anything but cherished. Special.

Had anyone ever told Caroline how special she was? Not for what she accomplished—she'd likely had commendations aplenty for her grades, her skills, her ability to make money. But had she ever felt the glow of being loved simply for who she was, her valor, her refusal to give up, her strength?

Lobo whined and stood up. Diego snapped from his reverie and saw his grandmother approaching. He rose and went to meet her. "I would have come to pick you up, *Abuela*."

She took his arm. "A walk in the evening does one good."

"May I get you something to drink?"

She smiled. "A glass of water would be welcome."

Diego settled her in the companion rocker and got her drink, wondering what she wanted. Mama Lalita did nothing without a purpose.

When she didn't speak but simply gazed out over the land, he sat down again and resigned himself to waiting. As the moments drew out, she placed one hand on his, and the peace that was so much a part of her seeped into him and eased his unrest.

"You are troubled, *m'ijo*."

He avoided that eagle's gaze. "Just tired."

Her hand squeezed his. "You work very hard, but you are making a difference, Diego. Yet as much as I wanted you here to care for the people, I never wanted you to suffer."

He frowned. "You've worked hard all your life. I'm not complaining."

"Of course not. You are a good man. These people badly need what you have to offer, but—"

"But what?"

For the first time in memory, he saw uncertainty on his grandmother's face. "We are keeping you from your heart," she said. "And I think the cost is too high." Her eyes were troubled when she faced him. "I would not have asked you to stay, if I had known." Her hands rose from her lap in a helpless gesture. "Now you are here, and so many come to you. I do not know what is to be done, Diego. And for that, I am deeply sorry."

The sight of tears in the eyes of the strongest woman he'd ever known shocked him. He slid forward, clasping both her hands in his. "I am where I belong, *Abuelita.*" He spoke past the ache in his own heart. "There is nothing to be done about…the other." He knew better than to deny Caroline's impact to his grandmother. So he shrugged. "I'll get past it."

She lifted workworn hands to his face. "You have conquered much, survived much, *m'ijo,* but this is different. She is part of you, and you will survive, yes, but you will not be whole without her. Nor she without you.''

He tried to pull away from her piercing gaze, but she held on. ''What would you have me do?'' he whispered. ''I can't leave here, and I can't ask her to give up her life there.'' And the fury and hurt of it would be choked back no more. ''Anyway, if she felt as I do, she wouldn't have left.''

Wise old eyes softened. ''Your world changed when she came. Perhaps hers is changed, as well. The answer to your question might be different now.''

''I can't ask it, *Abuela*. I know what she would be giving up.'' At that moment, he could have bitten off his tongue for letting the last dregs of bitterness through. ''I'm sorry.''

''Don't be,'' Mama Lalita said. ''Do you not think I understand how much was taken from you?''

''It doesn't matter now.''

''It does. Perhaps it always will.''

''No.'' He shook his head and dislodged her hands, rising to look into the distance. ''I won't let it.'' He bowed his head, then straightened again. ''What's done is done, *Abuela*.'' He turned to face her. ''I was supposed to be in a wheelchair, but I'm walking. I have many friends. I have patients who need me.'' He came to her then, crouching in front of her. ''I have love in my life, plenty of it. It's

galed him with the story that was already traveling hospital corridors at warp speed.

Miracle Malone was on her way back.

An impromptu celebration convened at the bar across the street from Mercy. It was far past her usual bedtime when Caroline got out of the cab Sam had insisted on procuring for her. He'd drive her, he said, but he himself had better be taking a cab.

He'd escorted her to the vehicle and handled her into it like fine crystal, leaving her with a big kiss smack on her lips. She had orders to report to Don's office first thing in the morning for a revised therapy plan. Don said that in this case, first thing should be considered noon. He'd been at the party, too.

Actually, she hadn't needed to drink much; her excitement had been its own buzz. Caroline waved to the cabbie from her doorstep, relieving him of Sam's charge. She let herself inside, blinking against the light.

Everything looked just the same as she'd left it. How could that be, when so much else had changed?

She locked the door and laid her things on the refectory table she'd spent so much time searching for. In the mirror above it, she stared at her reflection, lifting her right hand into view.

The fingers of her left hand traced its outline as

she strove to see it as it was, not as she'd viewed it for so many months: ugly...despicable for its weakness. She held it higher and tried to extend her fingers. With the brace, they could function fairly well; even without it, they no longer hung like so many broken sticks, if not yet normal.

It was not the hand that had once worked miracles. She had a long way to go. She'd seen the worried look in Don's eyes when Sam had predicted that she'd be doing procedures on her own by Halloween. Pulling back a flap of skin with a retractor or suctioning blood was a long way from wielding a scalpel.

But it was a start. For a moment, she closed her eyes and let the remembered smells and sounds of the O.R. filter in. She'd been half-alive since the accident, except when—

Her head dropped. She wouldn't think about Diego tonight. Tonight was for celebration.

Tossing back the hair she still hadn't gotten cut into her customary short cap, Caroline headed for the kitchen to make tea. She was wide-awake, but if she was to get started right tomorrow, she needed rest. She still had Adelaida's tea hoarded. Many a sleepless night she'd been tempted to use it, but she had so little left. She had only to open the tin and sniff and she felt close to them again. Not so lonely for a few precious moments.

She shuffled through her mail and came upon an

envelope addressed in Ivy's beautiful penmanship. Ivy—she could call her sister and tell her about today and the surgery and—

Caroline glanced at the clock. It was after midnight, and Amelia still woke in the night to feed. Ivy needed her sleep.

Caroline prolonged the pleasure of reading Ivy's letter as she put on water for tea. She smiled; she couldn't remember the last time she'd written a personal letter in this era of e-mail, but Ivy stubbornly clung to time-honored ways, bless her, never mind that they spoke on the phone often. Linc was trying to lure her to the Internet, but so far Ivy was holding firm.

Suddenly, looking around at the cool, pale colors she'd once thought perfect, contrasting them with the explosion of hues in Ivy's world, Caroline felt anew the pierce of loneliness. Maybe she'd go see them this weekend. It was too quiet around here. Maybe she'd think about getting that dog.

Memories of fat Dulcita and majestic Lobo crowded in, making way for thoughts of Lobo's lone-wolf owner. Lost in remembrance, she startled at the knock on her door.

Who on earth? Had Sam sent someone to make sure she'd arrived home safely?

She peered through the glass and stopped in shock.

It couldn't be.

Then she heard the voice from her dreams.

"It's late. Should I go?"

She yanked the door open, still trying to absorb that Diego was really here.

"No, no—come in, please." She shut the door behind him, leaning against it and staring at him, suddenly at a loss for words. He seemed weary and was even leaner than before.

But he looked wonderful to her.

They spoke at the same time.

"What are you—"

"How have you—"

Both stopped. Both smiled.

"You are still beautiful, *querida*." In that much-missed voice was a caress. "How are you?"

Her gaze dropped to those hands that had mesmerized her from the first. All at once, her house didn't feel so lonely. As always, his presence filled the room.

"I'm...good," she said. Then she remembered and grinned. "Better than good—I assisted in surgery today."

Diego's heart faltered. His trip had been for nothing. "That's...great. I'm glad for you." He tried his best to feel it.

Color stained her cheeks. "Yeah, well...I'm a long way from ready to crack a chest on my own."

"You will be." He didn't doubt it.

Her head rose; her eyes filled with a fragile hope.

"I'm going to try." Then her forehead creased. "Why are you here, Diego?"

For you. I came for you. But he couldn't say that now. He seized on the first thing that leaped to mind. "Looking for more equipment."

"How's the stuff that Mercy sent working out?" she asked.

"You didn't get my letter?"

She nodded. "Sam appreciated it."

I didn't write it for Sam, he thought. "So... things are going well."

Her slender shoulders lifted. "Yeah, great. How's Adelaida?"

"She sends you her love." He smiled. "And another tin of tea, which is in my truck."

"Oh—" Caroline straightened. "Where are my manners? You want something to drink or eat or—"

He almost said no. Almost took the opening to escape from the ache of being with her, now that he knew she was lost to him for good.

But something in him couldn't let go of her just yet. "Sure. Whatever you've got is fine."

That mouth he'd loved to kiss turned up in a smile sparkling with mischief. "I was just making some of her tea. You'd better go get your bag and be prepared to spend the night, though. It always seemed to put me down for a minimum of twelve hours."

He chuckled, trying not to think about spending the night, though it had been on his mind every inch of the past seven hundred miles. "I think I'll pass."

Spend the night. The phrase echoed through Caroline's brain. She couldn't take her eyes off him, drinking in his presence as though he were water and she'd been lost in the desert for weeks.

Water. His spring. "Diego, I'm sorry about the way I left. I just—"

He shook his head and lifted one hand to caress her cheek. "I understood. I wasn't asleep." His eyes met hers, and she felt the burn of tears. He'd let her go, knowing—

His thumb slid beneath her lashes, blotting the moisture as it fell. He lifted his hand and tasted the salty drops. "I knew you had to leave, *mi corazón.* You had to return and try again. It's who you are."

"Is it?" she whispered, staring at him. Wishing he'd touch her again. She took a step toward him, heart in her throat, but stopped short. "Diego, I— I missed you."

"Ah, Caroline…" Diego closed the distance, enfolded her in his arms. She leaned against him, clutching his shirt, resting against the bulwark of his solid strength. "I missed you so much," she murmured into his shoulder, free, now that he was here, to feel just how true it was.

His arms tightened on her, his body curving over

hers. "And I you, *querida*." His voice was rough. "But I'm glad you've regained what you lost."

"Are you?"

"Of course." Diego wanted to mean it, even though it signaled the death of his hopes.

Her head tilted back, and solemn green eyes studied his. "Thank you."

Diego looked at her mouth and knew he had to leave quickly. He didn't feel noble, no matter what he said. He'd let her go once, and it would kill him to do it again. He had to, for her sake, but damn if he could stand here and pretend it didn't hurt like hell.

He stepped away from her. "It's late. You need your sleep."

"But you just got here. Are you hungry?" She glanced around. "I don't keep much food stocked, but I could—"

"No." He clenched his jaw. "I'm fine. It was good seeing you, Caroline." He jerked his gaze away from the hurt in her eyes, heading for the door.

"Do you—would you like to stay here?" she asked in a small voice.

His knuckles went white on the doorknob. "I don't think so. Goodbye, Caroline." The knob slipped in his damp palm.

"Diego—" She moved up beside him and

touched his arm. "What is it? Why are you angry with me?"

"I'm not angry." He twisted the metal and yanked hard. Took a step outside. Heard his grandmother's voice. *Her answer might be different this time.*

Screw nobility. He whirled. "Hell, yes, I'm angry—" He abandoned all pretense of fairness. He was a healer, but he was a warrior, as well. "I should be glad because I care about you and it's what you want." He stared at her. "But I'm not. I don't want you here—I want you with me. I need you, and you know you need me, if only you'd stop being so scared."

She only looked at him, eyes huge in her face.

He swore and brushed past, pacing, raking fingers through his hair. "I understand what you're thinking. It makes no sense for you to come back— don't you think I've reasoned it out, six ways from Sunday?" Frustration ripped through him. "You've got everything you ever wanted right here. You've worked hard to succeed against all odds. There's nothing for you back there except a broken-down soldier and sure poverty."

He stopped in front of her, as if daring her to argue. "I know all the reasons it's wrong to take you back with me, but I want you, damn it—in my house and my bed and my life. I want to practice medicine with you and make babies with you—"

Caroline watched him, hands jammed in his pockets, eyes crackling with fury and—oh God— what looked like love and need.

And she understood then why nothing had fit since the day she'd returned. Why it never truly would. Because she'd left the best part of herself back in that valley, with simple people who'd taken her to their hearts.

With a man who had, for the first time in her life, made her whole. Found her enough.

But could it last? How could she risk it?

"I located Ivy," she blurted. "She was looking for me, too."

"What?" He stared at her as though she'd spoken a foreign language, then shook his head, disappointment shadowing his eyes.

"She's married and has a baby girl." Caroline's lips curved. "Named after me."

"I'm happy for you." He sounded anything but.

Caroline touched his arm. "I might never get it back, all the way."

"What?" He turned, frowning.

"My hand."

"What's that got to do with Ivy or—" Frustration simmered in his eyes.

Caroline stepped back from him, colliding with the refectory table. She wrapped her arms around herself, grasping for a way to explain. "Ivy's husband, Linc, said that he'd been alone since he was

eighteen. He told me that it took Ivy to convince
him that needing others wasn't a weakness.''

Diego studied her and said nothing.

''I thought—'' Her voice shook a little. ''Medicine was the only place I ever felt like I belonged.
But even there, I made sure that others needed
me—I never let myself need them.''

Diego had gone very still.

Her chest rose with a deep inhalation. ''I told
myself that my mother's mistake was to need my
father too much, that the only sure way to survive
was to be so strong that you didn't lean on anyone
else. If I was the best and I never needed anyone,
I'd be safe. Then I got injured, and I wasn't the
best any longer. I was so afraid. I didn't know who
I was anymore. But something happened in your
valley.'' Her eyes rose to meet his. ''I met people
who didn't care if I was the best. They liked me
just for me, even though I was damaged. Your
grandmother was so kind. Your friends made me
feel at home. And you—'' She took a deep, shud-
dery breath. ''You scared me to death because you
made me feel too much. I was underwater and
drowning fast. I had to get out. I ran back to what
I knew. Just like you said—'' Her gaze wavered.
''I ran away.''

Diego frowned and started to speak.

She held up her hand and continued. ''But nothing was the same anymore. I didn't belong—'' Her

mouth twisted. "If I ever did." She moved, starting to pace. "And then Ivy showed up and acted as though we were still the same, as though we could just love each other. That it didn't have to be complicated. That love could make you strong, not weak."

She whirled. "Part of me wants to return to the valley and be with you, help you take care of those people, but it's not that simple. It can't be. I have a chance to use skills that I worked hard to learn. If I don't, aren't I copping out? Not everyone can do what I do. Don't I have an obligation—" Confusion darkened her eyes. Her voice dropped to a whisper. "Anyway, I'm a lousy risk for love. I don't know the first thing about it."

"You're wrong." Diego spoke then, seeing a glimmer of hope. *Thank you, Mama Lalita.* "All that passion for your patients says you know plenty about giving love—you're just afraid to ask for it." He crossed to her then, wanting his hands on her. "You don't have to ask me, Caroline. You've had my heart for a long time. I need you just as much as you need me." His grin was wry. "I'm no bargain, either, you know."

"You are," she murmured. "You're the best man I ever met."

Diego stifled a snort. "My family would tell you I'm moody as hell and stubborn to boot."

"You're not—or maybe you are, but you're so

much more,'' she said, lifting her hand to his cheek.

Diego closed his eyes and leaned into her touch, placing his hand over hers. ''We can find a way, if we want it badly enough. Maybe we commute, so you can keep your practice.'' He watched her to see her reaction.

''Commute between here and your valley?'' Her eyes narrowed in consideration.

''There are poor people here, too,'' he pointed out. ''Maybe we set up another clinic in Dallas. We hire people to help—you tap your connections for help with funding. Zane offered to contribute before. This time I'll say yes.'' He grinned. ''My savings are stretched about as far as they can go.''

''I've got money saved up.'' Her eyes had a far-off look. ''And I could hit up Sam and my partners. Linc has lots of money and he's a great guy. He might want to help out, too—'' She started to pace again.

Diego stopped her. ''Forget the clinics. First things first. Do you love me?''

Her face went pale. ''What do you think?''

''Stop it, Caroline. Don't dance around the question.'' He held her gaze. ''It's time for you to quit running. To take a leap and trust me to love you. I'm not your father. You don't have anything to prove to me, but you've got to risk your heart or we don't have a chance. I want that chance, Caroline. I want you, more than I've ever wanted anything in my life.''

Fear squeezed her heart in a merciless fist. For a moment, she could barely breathe.

She stood very still and closed her eyes, letting the feel of his hand sweep through her, that warmth she'd missed so much. If she said the words, there was no turning back. She'd never been more afraid, not even as a teenage runaway stranded in a world turned ugly and dark.

''Look at me, *querida*.''

She did, seeing there all the answers to questions she'd been afraid to ask.

And she was not her mother. Even if Diego left her, she had proven she was strong enough to survive on her own.

''I won't leave you,'' he said as though he could hear her thoughts. ''I will cherish you and protect you to my dying breath. I will love you beyond the grave.''

Serious words from a serious man. A man of honor. A man to trust.

''You'd better,'' she said, trembling. ''You can't let me need you and walk away.''

Diego drew her closer than breath, nearer than a heart's beat. ''Say the words, *mi corazón*. Let your soul speak to mine.''

Lifting her face from the comforting warmth of his broad chest, Caroline rose to her tiptoes, halting with her lips an inch from his. "I love you, Diego Montalvo, and..." She hesitated, then took the leap. "And...I need you."

Diego closed his eyes in relief. "Thank you." Then he sealed his promise to her with a kiss that held the taste of a sacred vow.

EPILOGUE

"YOU DON'T REALLY have doubts, do you?" Ivy asked as she pinned Adelaida's lace *mantilla* to Caroline's now shoulder-length hair. "He's wonderful, Caroline. I love him already."

"You love everyone." Caroline met her sister's gaze in the mirror. Then she shook her head. "No. I'm nervous, but I love him. It's just that I wish—"

Blue eyes met green. "I know," Ivy said. "I thought we'd find Chloe by now, and we could be together today."

Caroline squeezed Ivy's hand. "We'll find her soon. Linc is one very determined man."

Ivy grinned. "Speaking of determined, Linc says Diego's been pacing on the porch. He's got his brothers on the lookout. He has this idea you might not show up."

"Oh, I'll show up." Caroline smiled back. "I've got too much invested in him now. Two clinics. Two staffs." She shuddered dramatically. "All that paperwork."

"Sam's been wonderful, though, hasn't he? Once he quit moaning about losing his rainmaker, he really got behind you. I've never seen a fund-raiser like him. I could have used him when I was trying to badger Linc into helping me rescue Palo Verde from withering away."

"Linc seems to think you did just fine on your own." They shared a laugh. Caroline rose and grasped Ivy's hands with both of hers.

Ivy glanced down at Caroline's right hand. "Sure it doesn't hurt?"

"Hardly at all. I removed an appendix without my wrist brace yesterday."

"Do you miss it? Being a hotshot cardiac surgeon?"

"I thought I would, but there's so much more in my life now. I like teaching, and I like breaking new ground, practicing medicine that incorporates the old ways and new." She smiled. "And Adelaida says I'm her second-best pupil."

"My sister the witch doctor," Ivy teased.

Caroline laughed, and Ivy clasped her in a hard hug. "Oh, I'm so happy to have found you. I missed you so much."

Ivy was free and easy with affection. Caroline wasn't, but she was learning. She leaned into her sister's embrace and felt the press of tears.

"Oh, don't—don't you dare." Ivy jumped back and dabbed at Caroline's cheeks with her handkerchief. "Grace and Jenna will kill me, after having to kidnap you to shop for this dress. Don't you dare spot it."

A knock sounded on the door. "You ready, ladies?" Linc's voice. He'd offered to escort Caroline down the aisle. Great-aunt Prudie, whom Ivy had discovered in Palo Verde, was tending Amelia, accompanied by Prudie's beau, Carl, were on baby-sitter duty with Amelia. "Your warrior isn't going to wait much longer," Linc said.

Her warrior. Caroline smiled. Her healer. The man who'd changed her life. "We're coming, Linc."

She watched as her sister's husband caught her in a quick but thorough kiss. She followed them, then waited at the edge of the porch with Linc, seeing her new family assembled. Her new life.

And there, by the spring where their hearts had first joined, she and Diego would join their lives.

Standing beside Diego, Jesse saw her first. His somber face creased in a smile, and he nudged his brother. When Diego spotted her, his shoulders visibly relaxed. He studied her with those sorcerer's eyes, and Caroline prayed never to awaken from the spell.

Here was love. Here was life. Here was home, now and forever.

I'm ready, she mouthed. Linc bent down as if to listen.

But Caroline had eyes only for the man who read her lips and smiled. No one else needed to hear. Her words, and her heart, were meant for only one man.

Diego.

Caroline was seized by the urge to run again, but this time there was a difference.

She would be running toward love, toward the future.

The past was over, and she was whole.

*   *   *   *   *

Be sure to look for the story of
Caroline and Ivy's sister, Chloe.
Coming in July 2003.

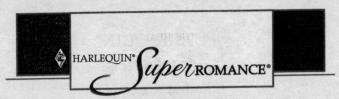

HARLEQUIN *Super*ROMANCE®

*presents a compelling family drama—
an exciting new trilogy
by popular author Debra Salonen*

THOSE SULLIVAN SISTERS

Jenny, Andrea and Kristin Sullivan are much more than sisters—*they're triplets!* Growing up as one of a threesome meant life was never lonely...or dull.

Now they're adults—with separate lives, loves, dreams and secrets. But underneath everything that keeps them apart is the bond that holds them together.

MY HUSBAND, MY BABIES
(*Jenny's story*)
available December 2002

WITHOUT A PAST
(*Andi's story*)
available January 2003

THE COMEBACK GIRL
(*Kristin's story*)
available February 2003

HARLEQUIN®
Makes any time special ®

Visit us at www.eHarlequin.com

HSRTSS

The world's bestselling romance series.

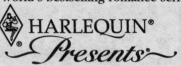

HARLEQUIN® Presents~

Seduction and Passion Guaranteed!

He's impatient... He's impossible...
But he's absolutely irresistible!
He's...

HER ITALIAN BOSS

Two original short stories to celebrate Valentine's Day, by your favorite Presents authors, in one volume!

The Boss's Valentine by Lynne Graham

Poppy sent Santiano Aragone a Valentine card to cheer him up. Santiano responded by making love to her... and suddenly Poppy was expecting her boss's baby!

Rafael's Proposal by Kim Lawrence

Natalie's boss, Rafael Ransome, thought she couldn't be a single mom and do her job. But then he offered her a stunning career move—a Valentine's Day marriage proposal!

HER ITALIAN BOSS
Harlequin Presents, #2302
On-sale February 2003

Pick up a Harlequin Presents® novel and you will enter a world of spine-tingling passion and provocative, tantalizing romance!

Available wherever Harlequin books are sold.

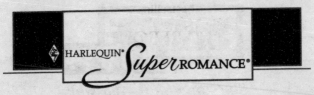

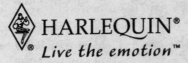

MAYBE BABY!

She's pregnant—possibly!

The possibility of parenthood: for some couples it's a seemingly impossible dream. For others, it's an unexpected surprise.... Or perhaps it's a planned pregnancy that brings a husband and wife closer together...or turns their marriage upside down?

One thing is for sure—life will never be the same when they find themselves having a baby...maybe!

This emotionally compelling miniseries from

HARLEQUIN®
Romance®

will warm your heart and bring a tear to your eye....

This month we bring you a wonderfully emotional story by RITA® Award-winning author

Lucy Gordon

Don't miss:

THE PREGNANCY BOND
on-sale January (#3733)

And look out for more
MAYBE BABY books
coming soon!

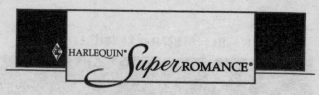

Welcome to Koomera Crossing,
a town hidden deep in the Australian Outback.
Let renowned romance novelist Margaret Way take
you there. Let her introduce you to the people of
Koomera Crossing. Let her tell you their secrets....

In **Sarah's Baby** meet Dr. Sarah Dempsey and
Kyall McQueen. And then there's the town's
matriarch, Ruth McQueen, who played a role
in Sarah's disappearance from her grandson
Kyall's life—and who now dreads Sarah's
return to Koomera Crossing.

Sarah's Baby is available in February
wherever Harlequin books are sold.
And watch for the next Koomera Crossing story,
coming from Harlequin Romance in October.

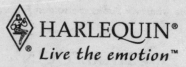

HARLEQUIN®
Live the emotion™

Visit us at www.eHarlequin.com

HARLEQUIN SUPERROMANCE®

HSRSBKC